A Very Happy Valentine

HAPPY EVER AFTER
BOOK TWO

ELISE NOBLE

Published by Undercover Publishing Limited

v4

ISBN: 978-1-912888-77-1

Edited by Nikki Mentges, NAM Editorial

Cover design by Elise Noble

www.undercover-publishing.com

www.elise-noble.com

All you need is love. But a little chocolate now and then doesn't hurt.

CHARLES M. SCHULZ

One

My name is Serena Carlisle, and I'm a fraud.

There, I said it.

I'm a fraud.

My brother passed the gravy, and I poured it over my roast potatoes.

"So, how's the new apartment?" he asked.

"On the small side, but it's in a great location. Only one street away from the Tube, and there are plenty of restaurants nearby."

"Did it come furnished?"

"It's rather minimalist, but I'll only be there for six months."

When I was eight years old, Kate Hodgson told me I could only sit at her lunch table if I was a vegetarian, and since Kate's mum was a yoga teacher and her dad was a TV chef and she was therefore the closest thing to a celebrity that Fairoaks Primary School had, I'd sworn blind that I didn't eat meat. Then I'd spent the next four years picking the ham out of my sandwiches on the way to the bus stop each morning, and even now, I still glanced behind me out of habit every time I bit into a burger.

I'd been pretending ever since.

Like now, for example. My new apartment in London was a dump. Seriously. I wouldn't have been surprised to see the roaches that lived under the kitchen sink packing their bags and moving out. By "minimalist," I meant that the only furniture was a coffee table with one leg shorter than the others, a single bed, and a musty-smelling couch, the last two of which I'd covered in sheets because I couldn't bear to touch the actual fabric. And by "plenty of restaurants," I meant it was above a kebab shop and opposite a Chinese takeaway.

But it was within my budget, and that was the important thing.

"Six months is a long time without creature comforts," Liam said. "Sure you don't want me to bring some of your furniture? I could rent a van."

"No, no, it's fine. Honestly. London's a long drive."

"Only a couple of hours."

"Don't you have packing to do?"

"Tickets, money, passport, swimming trunks. It'll take me five minutes."

"What about actual clothes? Aren't you planning to leave the hotel?"

My brother glanced at his girlfriend, and her cheeks turned scarlet.

"No?" he said.

"Okay, okay, spare me the details."

Liam had been dating Marissa for a little over a year now, or a little over two years if you counted the initial one-night stand gone wrong. The "gone wrong" part had inadvertently been my fault, not that anyone had realised it at the time. Luckily, the hand of fate—and a broken hip—

had given them a happy ending. Our parents were thrilled. Thrilled and relieved. "Marissa's remarkably normal," Mum had told me. "Not the kind of girl I thought Liam would end up with at all." Of course, the "normal" comment had come two days before Marissa realised she'd won the bloody lottery. Now they were off to the Caribbean to get some winter sun.

"We're staying in a suite," she said. "I only booked a regular room, but Mrs. Finnegan's niece works at the hotel, and she finagled us an upgrade. There's meant to be a whirlpool tub and a coffee machine."

You wouldn't know Marissa was a multimillionaire. Apart from the fact she'd taken driving lessons and upgraded her bicycle to a Volkswagen Polo, her life had barely changed. She still worked part-time in a care home because she liked chatting with the old folks, she shopped for yellow-label items at Tesco, and half of her clothes came from Vinted. Old habits died hard, she said, although Liam mentioned she'd donated a tidy sum to the cat rescue they'd adopted their new kitten from. The shoelace-obsessed little furball eyed up my feet from across the room, and I tucked them farther under my chair.

"Have you met Marc yet?" Marissa asked.

"He's flying in tomorrow."

"Are you nervous?"

I waved a hand. "Nervous? Oh, no, I've met so many actors that they all start to look the same."

Yes, I'd managed to turn my talent for faking it into a career. Not a particularly illustrious one, if I was honest, at least until three years ago, but I'd gone from regional theatre to three seasons of playing a ditzy police constable on *Whispers in Willowbrook*. The BBC mystery drama looked good on my CV, even if my job was far less glamorous than most people imagined. Early mornings, late nights, a lot of sitting around in the converted double-decker bus that served as our rest area in between scenes.

But on Boxing Day, I'd received the best slightly late Christmas present ever—a phone call from Patrick Sheridan. Visionary, acclaimed playwright, and last year's Tony Award winner for Best Director of a Play. And he'd wanted me to audition for a job.

Me!

Apparently, he was a big fan of British crime drama.

It wasn't such a great Christmas for Virginia Portman, who'd tripped and broken her leg while leaving a party on Christmas Eve, or her stand-in, who'd gone down with glandular fever, but I'd still danced around my cottage when I hung up the phone. Then stubbed a toe on a chair. It was at that point I considered that maybe the production of *The Other Woman* was jinxed, but I couldn't afford to turn down work. Acting didn't pay much. Usually, I recorded audiobooks in the off months when I wasn't communing with corpses, because the bills wouldn't pay themselves.

The Other Woman didn't have much of a budget, but it did have Marc di Gregorio. Hollywood superstar, media darling, and old college roommate of Patrick Sheridan. He didn't want to get typecast, apparently, which was why he'd agreed to star in Patrick's play for peanuts instead of playing yet another action hero. The entire run was sold out already.

No pressure, then.

And Marissa didn't seem convinced by my blasé attitude.

"They all look like Marc di Gregorio? But *Imagine* magazine said he was one of a kind. Do you think you'll be able to get us backstage passes?"

"That's not really a thing in theatre, but if we have a wrap party, you can definitely come as my date."

"I'm being ditched for my own sister?" Liam asked, but

he was smiling. "Speaking of parties, are you going to our high school reunion?"

Any joy I might have felt made a dash for the door, and the tension squeezing my belly ratcheted up a notch. Some fool in Liam's year had gone all American and decided Fairoaks Grammar simply must have a high school reunion. Except because our classes were relatively small, she'd invited the two years above and the two years below to make up the numbers. Unfortunately, that included me.

"No, I'm not."

"Because of the Carrie thing?"

The Carrie thing. Liam made it sound so innocuous, but having blood thrown over me at the school prom had been anything but trivial to eighteen-year-old me. I'd been ridiculed, I'd been arrested, and I'd lost a good friend over the incident.

"Yes, because of the Carrie thing."

"That was just one night."

"A night that ruined my life."

Of course Liam wouldn't understand. He'd always been one of the popular kids.

"Libby Sieber probably won't even go. I heard she's in the middle of a nasty divorce."

"Really? Well, she always did have terrible taste in men."

Our feud had started when she accused me of flirting with her boyfriend, which was crazy, and I told her so. Darren Hendon was a creep. The last thing I'd wanted to do was attract his attention.

Despite her constant sniping, I'd actually been looking forward to the prom. The end-of-year bash at a local golf club promised a chance to dress up, to say goodbye to old classmates, and to sample the results of the "design a graduation cocktail" contest, even if alcohol had lost some of its allure once I was old enough to buy it legally.

In hindsight, I should have realised that fate was trying to send me a message. First, a shop assistant had torn my dream dress while trying to remove a stubborn security tag, then I'd accidentally dyed my hair orange, and before I could beg a local stylist to fix the problem, Damon Clarke dumped me in a row over popcorn—we'd split the cost of a tub fifty-fifty, but apparently, I'd eaten more like seventy percent. Never mind the fact that I hadn't wanted to see the millionth instalment of the Fast and the Furious anyway, but— Whatever. Why hadn't I taken the hint?

Stupid, stupid me.

Instead of tearing up my prom ticket and acting as if I'd never wanted to go in the first place, I'd sniffled down the phone to my friend Owen, and Owen had felt sorry enough for me that he'd offered to drive back from university and pretend to be my date. Owen, the nerd who'd never quite fitted in at Fairoaks Grammar either. Owen, who'd spent hours helping me with my homework when he used to live next door. Owen, who'd moved to Cambridge to study computer science on a full scholarship and left a gaping hole in my life. He'd even promised to hire a tuxedo.

I should have said no.

I should have eaten a pint of chocolate ice cream and cried over Netflix.

I should have bought one of those customised voodoo dolls with Damon's face and burned it on a tiny funeral pyre.

But instead, I'd tearfully accepted Owen's offer, then been forced to avoid him forever when his rented tuxedo got ruined and Libby and her cronies turned on him too. The last time I'd seen him, he was on the phone with my parents, trying to explain why I was being loaded into the back of a police van.

Did you know it's possible to get expelled after your final exam? No, neither did I.

"You should consider going to the reunion," Liam said. "Hold your head high. I bet you've done better for yourself than all those idiots who used to hang out with Libby."

A year ago, my answer would have been "No way," but today, a finger of smug satisfaction poked me in the forehead. Libby Sieber was going through a bad break-up while I was footloose, fancy-free, and about to star in a play with one of Hollywood's hottest properties. There would be a ton of PR, and didn't dumb-ass reporters after a story always spread rumours of romance between colleagues? Lucas Collins had held a door open for me at an awards ceremony once, and the next thing I knew, there was a picture of the two of us on Twitter. *Serena's secret smile—is romance on the cards for Detectives Cartwright and Hosier?* Although I'd watched most of his movies, I'd only ever said one word to him—"thanks"—and if I remembered rightly, the smile had been because I could finally go back to the hotel and get out of my awful bloody heels. And I'd only been there because Viola, my ride-or-die bestie through theatre school who'd decided she preferred being backstage, had been nominated for Best Hair & Make-up.

"Technically, I didn't graduate," I told Liam. "I'd feel like a fraud."

"It's not an official school event. And you passed your exams, didn't you? That's what matters."

"Fine, I'll think about it. Can you send me the link to the Facebook group? I deleted it."

Liam nodded. "Go show them that you made something of yourself. My famous big sister."

Marissa reached across the table and squeezed my hand. "Liam might not say it often, but he's so proud of you."

As it always did, a guilty chill ran through me because all

I did was pretend. *Pretend to be a cop. Pretend people's judgment didn't bother me. Pretend to be happy.* Liam was an actual doctor. He saved people in real life while I faked it on TV.

But just as I'd practised a hundred times, I acted coy and smiled.

"Thanks, little bro. I'm proud of you too."

"Happy New Year."

He held up his glass in a toast, and I clinked it.

"Let's hope it's a good one."

Two

"They're here!" the stage manager announced.

The costume designer began fanning herself, and across the room, Priscilla Prentice closed her copy of the script and sat up straighter. Priscilla was playing Eliza, my competition in *The Other Woman*, and it seemed the animosity extended off stage because so far, she'd been decidedly cool towards me. Probably because I'd taken her friend's role. She and Virginia Portman had been pals since they shared the role of Matilda in the West End musical.

The concept of the play was simple but quirky. We'd play two women competing for the same man, and at the end of Act Three, the audience would vote on the ending they wanted to see. On which of us would get Marc. Sorry, I meant Richard. My mistake. The marketing team had billed it as "a captivating and emotionally charged play that delves into the complexities of love, loyalty, and the power struggles that arise within relationships," and tickets were changing hands for twice their face value on the resale sites. Possibly because Marc took his shirt off in the second act.

Two weeks to rehearse, one month to perform. We weren't quite in the West End, but we weren't a million miles away. Sticking with the "quirky" theme, Patrick Sheridan had chosen a theatre in Dalston, a former Art Deco-style cinema saved from demolition and turned into a performance space. Rehearsals were in a shuttered primary school along the street, and that place *would* be meeting the wrecking ball in a few months. So for now, we were sitting on tiny chairs, surrounded by corkboards covered in faded drawings of cats and rainbows while we waited for Marc and Patrick to grace us with their presence.

My palms began to sweat, and my phone slipped out of my hand. Dammit! It bounced off my foot and came to rest beside Andi, one of the stagehands, and of course she glanced at the screen as she handed it back to me.

"OMG! Marc di Gregorio split up with his girlfriend?"

"Maybe? I mean, that's what the story says."

Priscilla's perfectly plucked eyebrows pinched together. "Are you on that awful gossip site? They lie about everything."

"Uh, I was just curious."

And perhaps I was also signed up for celebgossip.com's free newsletter. *The Daily Dirt* promised to dish the good stuff before anyone else. Forewarned was forearmed, after all.

"Some of what they write is true," Andi said. "They broke the news of Scott Lowes's wedding. Broke my freaking heart too."

"They said Virginia split up with Terrence, and that's not true."

"Are you sure?" the property master asked. "I got a buddy who works in the same investment bank as Terrence, and he said Terrence took a job in the Dubai office."

"It's only temporary," Priscilla snapped. "They're on a break."

The guy held up both hands. "Okay, whatever you say."

"I do say, so why don't you keep your nose out of—" Her scowl morphed into a sultry smile. "Patrick! How was your flight?"

And there he was. Marc di Gregorio, in the lightly tanned flesh. He was shorter than I'd imagined—his bio said six feet, and he was more like five-ten—but even more handsome in person. A chiselled jaw, artfully dishevelled chestnut hair, and the type of smile that went *ping* in a toothpaste advert. And it wasn't just his physical features that drew attention. Marc di Gregorio had an aura that screamed "look at me," the kind of confidence that I'd never been able to fake, no matter how hard I tried.

Patrick was the same age—thirty-two—but his hair had greyed out, and the fine lines around his eyes made him look older. His smile was kind rather than sinful. The two of them weren't alone, either. A film crew trailed behind them, and I swallowed a groan. My agent had explained that a producer friend of Patrick's was putting together a "Making of" documentary, but I'd hoped they might wait until after the introductions to start recording everything.

No such luck.

And the people kept coming. A make-up artist, a beefy guy I assumed was a bodyguard, several assistants... Soon, the old school hall was bursting at the seams. The make-up artist paused to study me and tutted a little. What did that mean? My skin was too pale? My dark hair was too thick? Or had she noticed the worry lines on my forehead?

"The flight was delayed by an hour," Patrick said.

Marc seemed the most relaxed out of all of us. "They told us it would be two hours, so we ordered dinner, and then we had to board before we finished the appetiser."

We lived in different worlds. My dinner had been a Tesco sandwich as I read through the script for the hundredth time. We had a basic storyline to follow, but Patrick encouraged us to put our own spin on the roles. Having to improvise was worse than following precise directions—so many new ways to go wrong.

Marc looked at me, and then he glanced at Priscilla. His trademark smile didn't waver as he stepped forward, but my heart hop-skip-jumped when he kissed me on the cheek.

"Serena Carlisle... I'm a huge fan of your work."

"You are?"

"British crime drama is a guilty pleasure." His grin grew wider, and he pointed his fingers like a pair of manicured pistols. "Cracking cases, one cuppa at a time?" Wow, he knew Detective Cartwright's catchphrase? "Tell me they didn't really kill you off?"

"They haven't made a final decision yet."

In last season's finale, Detective Cartwright had been kidnapped by a maniac, and when the closing credits rolled, she'd been lying motionless in a cellar with blood trickling from her mouth. Nobody yet knew whether she'd live or die, including me.

"If they cut you loose, they'll regret it. Trust me." He turned to my co-star, and she quickly schooled her frown into a smile. "You must be Priscilla?"

She leaned in and offered her cheek. "I've just finished a run in the West End."

"Congratulations."

Patrick clapped his hands together. "Thanks to the delays at the airport, we're already over an hour behind, so let's finish the intros and get to work. Folks, meet Chris Barnett —he'll be producing the documentary that runs alongside the play, and before we left LA, we agreed to a distribution deal with one of the streaming services. They want the whole package—the play, both endings, and the 'Making of.' Don't plan on getting much sleep over the next six weeks. Feather has put together a rehearsal schedule"—Feather?—"although that needs to change to accommodate the lost time."

A waif with a nose ring and pink hair styled in a pixie cut stepped forward. "Uh, I already laminated them."

"Then you'll need to laminate more."

"Or maybe you could email an update?" I suggested. "Thinking of the planet and everything."

"I need a hard copy," Priscilla said.

Of course she did. Guess she wasn't much of an eco-warrior.

"If we all stay an extra hour tonight, wouldn't that put us back on track?" I suggested.

Patrick shook his head. "We're going out for dinner tonight, and the table is booked for eight. Moving on, this is Carla McIntyre. Carla's a psychologist attached to the University of Coastal California, and she'll be writing a paper on the impact of demographics on relationship decisions. *The Other Woman* isn't just a play, it's a fascinating study of the human psyche, don't you agree? Will an audience with a higher percentage of men make a different decision than one skewed toward women? Is age a contributing factor? How about relationship status?"

"Will people want to answer those questions?" Priscilla asked.

"It's an immersive experience. Only those who fill out the questionnaire will be eligible to vote on the final act."

"Audience members can remain completely anonymous," Carla explained. "But if they do choose to leave their details, one lucky winner will receive a signed copy of the script at the end of the run."

"What if they lie?" the sound engineer asked. "When my wife turned forty, she started counting backward."

"It's how a person identifies that's important."

"You're as old as the woman you feel," Marc quipped, and everyone except Priscilla laughed. But my laughter quickly faded as I read down the schedule Feather handed me. Patrick hadn't been kidding when he said our lives would be his for the next six weeks—not that I minded, because I needed to pay my rent—and I didn't love the idea of walking home from the Tube station at midnight. And wait, *I* was expected to go to dinner tonight? There it was in black and white: *Icebreaker @ Sushi in the City (Patrick, Marc, Priscilla, Serena)*. I mean, I hadn't been looking forward to cooking, mainly because the microwave was one spark away from a meltdown, but a cosy meal with Marc di Gregorio had never been a part of my plan. The knot of tension in my stomach pulled tighter, but hadn't I wanted this? Hadn't I wanted to be seen with Mr. Hollywood?

Patrick smacked him on the back. "Then you're perpetually twenty-one, buddy."

"Twenty-five. A little maturity can be sexy."

Maturity? Seriously? I was twenty-six, and some days, I was amazed I managed to put my shoes on the right feet. When I hit fifty, would I finally feel like a grown-up? Sometimes, being an adult sucked. The responsibilities, the expectations, the bills... If they ever did a remake of *13 Going on 30*, then I was the girl for the role. Carla was studying Marc closely. Did her professional curiosity extend beyond the audience?

I sure hoped not. The idea of being scrutinised by not only the film crew and the audience but also a woman who might see through my act made the hairs on the back of my neck prickle.

A lady in a suit cleared her throat and cut her eyes

towards the cameraman. She looked like a lawyer. Was she a lawyer? Image consultant? The morality police? Nobody clarified, but Patrick checked his laminated schedule and then his watch.

"Act One, Scene One. We need Richard and Eliza."

Three

"Could I just get a picture?" a pretty redhead asked.

Sushi in the City was a tiny slice of Japan in London, not too far from Leadenhall Market. The only people who could afford to eat there were investment bankers and the generationally wealthy—I'd found that out a year ago when a chap I met on Tinder insisted it would be the perfect place for our first date. He spent three courses and wine telling me how he was all for equality, then expected to split the bill right down the middle. Which would have been expensive but understandable if he hadn't picked the priciest bottle of red on the menu, drunk three-quarters of it himself, and then washed it down with three shots of top-shelf sake. And a lack of self-awareness was the least of his problems.

I cringed at the memory—I'd only been staying in London for a few days, and all I'd wanted was some company, but instead I'd ended up walking back to my hotel because I couldn't afford the Tube fare.

At least tonight, the fancy setting and the mâitre d'-slash-samurai guarding the door meant we hadn't been bothered too much during the meal, not in person anyway. It had been hard to miss the people taking pictures while they pretended to check their phones, and one blonde had even done a not-too-subtle TikTok live. But finally, a diner had been brave enough to ask Marc for an autograph, and that opened the floodgates. All through dessert, a steady stream of people had sidled up to the table, scraps of paper in hand. Marc took the requests with good grace, and Patrick seemed happy because, as he never stopped reminding us, no publicity was bad publicity. Priscilla had been prickly from the moment we sat down, and her irritation only increased as Marc posed for selfies. At first, I thought she was annoyed at the constant interruptions, but then I realised the opposite was true—she was peeved that somebody else was the centre of attention. When a couple asked her to take a picture of them with Marc and me, she clenched her jaw so hard I thought she'd crack a tooth.

Thankfully, the redhead was the last of the selfie hunters, and this time, I offered to play photographer because according to Feather's schedule, Priscilla didn't have time for emergency dental work. We'd be rehearsing twelve hours a day for the next two weeks. I'd even overheard Andi whispering about bringing a sleeping bag to work with her.

"Is it always like this?" I asked when the redhead had gone back to her table.

"Once you become better known, yes," Priscilla told me before Marc could get a word in edgeways. "Fame can be bittersweet." Had she practised that condescending smile in the mirror? "Perhaps someday you'll experience it for yourself."

In the play, the two of us were rivals—my character, Alice, was a paralegal who'd been forced out of a City law firm after Eliza had taken a dislike to her. And now life was imitating art. I *wanted* to like Priscilla because if we all got along, the next six weeks would be a heck of a lot easier. But I was struggling.

Support came from an unexpected source.

"You'd be surprised how many people in LA have heard of Serena," Marc said, then turned to me. "Enjoy the peace while you can. If twenty-year-old me had realised what a blessing anonymity was, I'd have spent more time in the grocery store. Hell, maybe I'd have chosen to work there."

"You don't like your job?"

"I love my job. The bullshit that comes with it? Not so much."

"Promo's a necessity, folks," Patrick reminded us. "Even a passion project has to cover its costs."

And the rent.

And the aforementioned groceries.

Priscilla beamed at him. "I'm happy to do all the promo you want, Patrick."

"Good to hear. In this industry, it's important to be a team player."

I should have volunteered as well, I knew I should, but I couldn't bring myself to utter the words. *Fraud, fraud, fraud.* I didn't even love my job—I'd just accidentally found something I was good at, and for a girl who'd barely scraped through her A-levels, theatre school had represented the best chance of earning a living wage.

I agonised over the "team player" point while a server dressed as Hello Kitty slid bowls of mochi and a selection of dorayaki pancakes in front of us, but before I could decide on the best course of action, Feather materialised beside Patrick, iPad in hand. Much whispering took place. I heard Marc's name mentioned and something about a tape.

My phone buzzed.

"Call Jessica," Patrick instructed, then gave his head a little shake. "Bro, you made a tape?"

My phone buzzed again.

"A tape?"

"With Soreen?"

Soreen? According to celebgossip.com, Soreen was the name of Marc's ex-girlfriend. I distinctly remembered that fact because it was also the name of the UK's favourite brand of malt loaf, and who on God's green earth would name their child that?

"Sure, we did a few read-throughs."

I couldn't stand it any longer. Nobody was paying me the slightest bit of attention anyway, so I slid the phone out of my pocket and glanced at the messages.

MARISSA

Have you seen this?

VIOLA

OMG that stud is hung!

"Not that kind of tape, you jackass," Patrick said. "A sex tape."

Priscilla began coughing. Good grief, did she always have to be so melodramatic?

"Oh, *that* tape. Soreen said she deleted it."

"Well, she didn't. It's all over BuzzHub."

"Does my dick look good?"

Now it was Patrick's turn to be melodramatic. He thunked his head on the table and groaned, although the groan was barely audible over Priscilla's retching. Wait a second... Was she actually choking?

Flipping heck, she'd gone bright red, and if Patrick lost another cast member, he'd probably lose his mind as well. Thankfully, Liam had been an enthusiastic medical student, and I knew all about abdominal thrusts. I leapt up, squeezed hard, and a piece of dorayaki pancake landed in the water jug.

Holy forking shirtballs. We'd already had a sex scandal and a near-death experience, and this was only day one of rehearsals.

Twenty minutes later, Priscilla had been loaded into the back of an ambulance, which she didn't need but insisted upon anyway. Feather had gone with her. I wasn't certain whether that was because Patrick thought Priscilla might need assistance or because Feather had started hyperventilating at the news of Dickgate. Patrick had been texting furiously since her departure, but now he'd switched to pacing near the bar, muttering to someone on the phone. Marc was spooning melted ice cream into his mouth. Me? I was trying to decide whether to click on the link Marissa had sent. I mean, it was undoubtedly poor etiquette to watch a colleague doing the nasty on the internet, but I was only human. And female. And hella curious.

"You seem remarkably relaxed about this," I said to Marc. "I thought you weren't keen on public scrutiny?"

"Can't put the genie back in the bottle. I can either accept the situation or have a nervous breakdown. Stress ages you, did you know that?"

Yes, I did. My first wrinkle had appeared after the Carrie incident. More of a frown line, really, but I'd risked Botox after snide comments from some of the girls at theatre school.

"I guess we're about to test Patrick's 'no publicity is bad publicity' hypothesis." I glanced across to the bar, where he was still pacing. "He seems more upset than you do."

Marc shrugged. "He's probably trying to work out how he can leverage this into a run on Broadway."

"Seriously?"

"That was always his goal, but nobody wanted to take a chance on a concept like this one." Marc finished his last mouthful and dropped the spoon into the bowl. "We should get some sleep. Do you have a ride home?"

"I'll just take the Tube."

"Is that safe?"

"Yes?"

"You don't sound certain. We'll give you a ride."

And have him see the hovel I was living in? No thanks.

"Honestly, I'll be fine."

"At least let me find you a cab."

Admitting to Marc di Gregorio that I couldn't really afford a cab would be worse than using my credit card to pay for one, so I nodded my agreement.

"Thanks, I appreciate it."

Marc did cover dinner, which was one less expense, plus he held the door open for me as we exited the restaurant. That little touch on the small of my back was just him being friendly, right? Ditto for the peck on the cheek as he helped me into a black cab. I'd known him for less than twenty-four hours, and he already had my stomach tied in knots. This wasn't my world. Serena Carlisle didn't do off-set drama.

My phone buzzed again as the cab pulled away, and I thought it would be another message from Viola, but no, my brother had added me to the school reunion group. I clicked on the link, more to stop myself from clicking on the *other* link than anything else. Finding out that Annette Sumner had married a lawyer was so much more civilised than checking out the size of Marc's anatomy.

The reunion ball had a Valentine's theme, hearts and flowers. One of the organisers said the venue was half the price on February fourteenth—probably because all the normal people were squashed into restaurants at tables for two—so they'd decided to spread the love and make it a combined event. Yeuch. I scrolled through the updates, the bragging, the gossip, the comments asking people if they were going to the party.

Then my heart stuttered.

Pete Wilkins: Piper, are you going?

Piper? That had been one of Owen's old nicknames. He was in the group? Almost unconsciously, my hand went to my necklace. It wasn't anything fancy, just a plastic gummy bear on waxed cord, but I'd worn it ever since he gave it to me. I'd been sixteen and miserable, dreading my parents' disappointment after collecting a D in my GCSE maths mock, but Owen had always found a way to make me smile.

Here's a little bear hug for when you're feeling blue.
Because bears are tough and so are you.

The necklace had come with a card, and now I slid it out of my wallet and studied the words, the edges worn from a decade of being carried around. Yes, I'd survive. I'd get through the next six weeks, no matter how much crap got slung my way.

A new comment appeared.

Owen Cadwallader: Don't call me that if you want me to answer.

Owen was sticking up for himself? Fifteen years ago, he'd accepted the nickname, even though he hated it. Like me, he'd always tried to fly under the radar, but after he won a local contest by reciting pi to 2,736 decimal places, the new moniker had been inevitable. *The Pied Piper.* His mum said everyone was just jealous of his mathematical ability, but I thought they were jealous that he also won a year's supply of pie from Sweet Treats, which, let's face it, was the best prize ever. We used to swing by the bakery every day after school to collect his goodies.

Pete Wilkins: Sorry, forgot you had a sense-of-humour bypass.

Owen Cadwallader: Or maybe none of your jokes were funny.

I clicked on Owen's profile, but he'd locked it down. Even the picture wasn't of him—it was a pi symbol. A joke? All through our teenage years, he'd been oh-so serious in public, but he had a deliciously dark sense of humour hidden away where few ever saw it. My finger hovered over the "add friend" button, but in the end, I closed the app.

Sometimes, it was better to let the past stay in the past.

Four

"Have you seen the latest?" Viola demanded the moment I picked up the phone.

"What time is it?" I groaned.

"Like, ten p.m.?"

Ten p.m. in LA? Dammit! Why hadn't my alarm gone off?

Probably because you forgot to set it, idiot.

"I'm late."

"Late for what?"

"Rehearsal."

"Isn't it, like, six a.m. over there?"

"Yes, but we're starting early."

"And you had a late night, right?"

"Not stupidly late. I was home by eleven and— Wait, how do you know I had a late night?"

"Because it's all over the internet? I can't believe you went on a date with Marc di Gregorio and you didn't tell me. What happened to 'sisters before misters'?"

"What? Why would you think I went on a date with Marc?"

"Because you were looking cosy over dinner? Because he had his hand on your arse? Because he kissed you?"

"What? None of that's true."

"There are pictures."

I grabbed my iPad and typed my name into the search bar, and oh my gosh... Viola wasn't kidding. There were pictures of Marc and me from last night, dozens of them, all carefully cropped to make them look like something they weren't. Patrick and Priscilla had disappeared from the table, the angle carefully selected to make Marc and me appear closer together than we actually had been. Ditto for the snap as we left the restaurant. His hand had definitely been on my back, but now it looked lower. And the peck on the cheek as I climbed into the cab seemed so much more intimate, probably because I had my freaking eyes closed.

"We went for a 'get to know each other' dinner with Patrick and Priscilla, but then Priscilla ended up in hospital, and Patrick had a meltdown, and this is all freaking lies. What am I meant to do?"

"Uh, breathing might be a good idea?"

I sucked in air. "I meant about the whole situation. Should I write something on social media?"

"No! If you deny it, then people will only believe it more."

"So I sit back and let everyone think I'm dating a serial womaniser?"

"I mean, things could be worse. At least Marc di Gregorio is hot."

"Viola, he just put out a sex tape!"

"Technically, I think his ex-girlfriend was the one who released it. Hell hath no fury like a woman scorned, right? Although he's definitely gonna come out the other side looking better than she does."

"You think?"

"Everyone knows Soreen Mickelhoff is an attention seeker. She's already recorded an episode for her podcast, and I hear she's booked on three talk shows this week so far. Have you watched the tape? There's not a woman on this planet who wouldn't want Marc di Gregorio licking her—"

"Please, it's too early for this." I struggled to my feet and swayed for a second. Mornings should be illegal.

"He might be a sex addict, but at least he's good at it. Are you sure you're not dating?"

"I think I'd know if we were."

Although... Did Libby Sieber read the gossip columns?

"But maybe there's a chance? You guys have chem-is-try. It shines through in the video." There was a video? Crap on a cracker. "True, his relationships last about two weeks, max, but it would help out with the whole dry spell, wouldn't it? How long has it been? Over a year, right? Who was that guy who grunted as he came? Dan? Don?"

"I'm going to hang up now."

"Call me if anything happens. Promise me. I can't believe you're in every gossip column and I'm five thousand miles away."

"Go to sleep."

"How can I sleep?"

"Try taking Benadryl."

"The drugstore closed an hour ago. Life officially sucks —you're hanging out with Marc di Gregorio and I have to camp out in deepest Wyoming."

"That 'end of civilisation' movie?"

"Death by killer fungus. I only hope there's indoor plumbing."

I tossed the phone onto the bed and sagged against the wall. A sex tape? Good grief. Nothing like this had ever happened on *Whispers in Willowbrook*. The closest we'd come to a scandal was when John Hillier, who played my boss, got arrested for drink-driving after he rear-ended a police car at a roundabout. Except it turned out he wasn't really drunk—he'd just had a bad reaction to his hay fever medication and got disorientated. Luckily, nobody was seriously hurt.

But this kind of rumour-gossip-scandal? It was in a whole other league. I was way out of my depth with *The Other Woman*, and I wouldn't be able to come up for air for six long, long weeks.

"How are you feeling?" I asked Priscilla.

"Fine."

If I'd expected gratitude for unblocking her airway, I'd been sorely mistaken. Priscilla seemed more annoyed with me than anything else. She didn't seem to have an issue with Marc, though. Today, the two of them were running through their scenes first while I watched and learned and desperately tried to get into Alice's head.

"How are *you* feeling?" Carla asked, sliding into the seat next to me.

Great. A shrink. That was the last thing I needed.

"Are you asking out of professional curiosity or concern for my well-being?"

She laughed. "Can't it be both?"

"I'm not thrilled to have people taking pictures of me all the time," I admitted.

"Why is that?"

"Because I value my privacy."

"And yet you chose a career that put you in the public eye."

"Bit of a mistake, that."

"Was it? One could argue that your career is going from strength to strength."

One could, if one treated the gossip rags as non-fiction. Yet somehow, I was still living alone in a one-bed flat in the arse end of town.

"I'm hardly a megastar. I'm just trying to pay the bills like everyone else, and acting is the only thing I was any good at."

"If you could turn back the clock, would you take a different path?"

"I... I'm not sure." Nobody had ever asked me that before. Everyone just assumed I was happy. "There's one moment—I guess you could say it was a defining moment—that I wish I could erase. And if that day had been different, I think my whole life would have been different. But what does it matter? I'm a pawn in a game of chess. No backwards, only forwards."

Carla leaned in closer. "It's not a breach of ethics to tell you that your colleagues don't think of themselves as pawns. Be a queen instead, and then you can move anywhere you please."

"It's not that easy."

"Only if you never try."

"Are you a psychologist or a life coach?"

"Both. Coaching pays the bills, but research is my passion."

What was my passion? I didn't have one, not unless you counted M&S profiteroles, which wasn't an addiction I'd ever admit to in interviews. No, I just said "my work *is* my passion" or something else suitably trite.

"I'll give it some thought."

Carla merely smiled and opened her laptop.

Be a queen.

I held onto that thought during my first scene with Marc, and no matter how much of a car crash his personal life was, the man could act. If I hadn't read the script and listened to Patrick's directions—*I want to feel the heat, people. Let the sparks fly*—I might have really believed that Marc was into me. The initial meeting, the cosy lunch our characters shared as Richard's apology for knocking Alice down in the street, the way his hand lingered on my arm as he finagled her number.

Then I was into a monologue, a call from Alice to her best friend. She gushed over meeting a great guy and puzzled over the fact that there was something familiar about him, but she couldn't quite put her finger on what. His face? His mannerisms? He'd denied meeting her before, so maybe she was imagining it? Her excitement that love might be just around the corner felt real, as did the horror when Alice finally realised where she'd seen him. Smiling from the photo on Eliza's desk.

Her ex-boss's desk.

The desk of the woman who'd fired her.

The honourable thing would have been for her to walk away, but the heat in her veins warred with the prospect of stone-cold revenge. Eliza had ruined her life, so why not return the favour?

Perhaps I was biased, but I believed I had the hardest job out of the three of us. Richard's heart would battle against his sense of morality, but the ultimate decision lay with the audience. Would they choose Eliza or Alice? Eliza was a career woman whose sense of worth depended upon her professional achievements. Work came before her personal life. She was the breadwinner, the provider, generous with money but not with time. How many people would see a reflection of their own relationship in Richard and Eliza?

Alice was the mistress, society's dirty little secret. Even after dreams of revenge turned into genuine affection, would the audience—the judge and jury—allow love to win over a ring? Would they react positively to the chemistry between Alice and Richard?

Only time would tell.

Time.

We had less than two weeks until the curtain went up.

That night, I lay in bed, wild thoughts running through my mind as I listened to idiots arguing outside the kebab shop below. But instead of thinking of one man who had no business being in my head, I found myself thinking of two. Marc and Owen. One a work colleague who made my thighs clench all of their own accord, the other the boy I'd been secretly in love with and then lost because, just for once, I'd gone with my heart rather than my head.

Marc's legal team had got the sex tape banned, but as he'd said yesterday, you couldn't put the genie back in the bottle. As fast as the videos got pulled down, more copies sprang up in their place. Soreen claimed to be a victim too—someone had stolen her phone, she said. Did I believe her? Not even a little bit. Those tears were over the top, and if she'd gone to the same theatre school as I did, she'd have failed the immersive performance class for sure.

Marc had posted a diplomatic statement—written by Jessica, the play's publicist—expressing disappointment that a private moment had been exploited and sympathy for poor

Soreen's plight. In private, he'd been royally pissed with her, but he had to play the game. We all did. Elegant swans on the surface, feet furiously paddling beneath the water to stay afloat. Although perhaps I was more of a duck.

Sleep eluded me, and I spent far more time googling the whole affair than I should have, at the same time thanking the stars that I wasn't the main subject of tonight's gossip. Clearly, the paparazzi had come to their senses and realised there was no way Marc would date a girl like me. When the articles started rehashing the same old rubbish, my mind wandered to the other upcoming clown show, and I checked in on the reunion group. This time, someone more polite had asked Owen if he'd be attending. His answer? *Probably not.* Two tiny words, but I wasn't prepared for the rush of emotion when I read them. Disappointment came first because if he wasn't there, I couldn't "accidentally" run into him, could I? But there was also relief, because now there was no reason for me to go to what Annette Sumner had dubbed the "Valentunion." Instead, I could spend my second evening of freedom after the play finished decompressing in my own bed, hopefully with a successful show to add to my acting résumé. No more Marc, no more Priscilla. Maybe the writers of *Whispers in Willowbrook* would be impressed by my success and Detective Cartwright would be found alive? Then I could go back to my regular, boring life and never darken Hollywood's doorstep again.

I should have turned off my phone.

I should have closed my eyes and counted sheep.

But like a fool, I kept doom-scrolling. Haylee Jacobs was offering anyone going to the reunion a twenty percent discount in her salon. Hair and aesthetics. I shuddered— after my foray into the world of Botox, which had left my face ever so slightly wonky for six freaking months, I'd vowed to grow old naturally.

Melinda Jones: Is Jonny Versey still in prison?

What? Jonny had gone to prison? Wow. The teachers had voted him "Most likely to succeed" in the end-of-year assembly, although I suspected they weren't aware he used to sell baggies of weed behind the bike shed at lunchtime. I quickly googled him. Oh. It seemed he *had* been quite the entrepreneur. Right up until the moment a police dog pulled him out of his Lamborghini by the seat of his pants, he'd run the biggest drugs ring in Surrey.

Rebecca Felton was using the opportunity to try and flog scented candles to a captive audience, and half a dozen people had left snotty comments telling her it wasn't the time or the place. Katie Briggs wanted to buy a candle. Arthur Willis posted a picture of a yacht in the Caribbean and said he couldn't make the reunion because he was going on holiday. His sister told everyone that he'd be spending a week in a caravan in Bognor, and Harvey Yorath ran a reverse image search and found the yacht actually belonged to a Russian oligarch.

Spying on my old schoolmates this way felt weird. A touch voyeuristic, but oddly satisfying.

Pepper Collins: Has anyone heard from Serena Carlisle? Is she coming?

Should I be flattered that someone had remembered I existed or uncomfortable that they were talking about me? Pepper Collins had been friendly with Libby, so definitely the latter.

Owen Cadwallader: After what you and Libby did to her at the school prom? I seriously doubt it.

Pepper Collins: I was only asking.

Owen Cadwallader: How about you try apologising instead?

After all these years, after everything that had happened, Owen was still defending me? I tried to swallow the lump in my throat, but it stubbornly stayed stuck. Wedged firm. I wanted to reach out and hug him through the screen, but the only thing I could do was hit the "like" button. Then I placed the phone face-down on the cardboard box that served as a nightstand, closed my eyes, and tossed and turned the whole night.

Five

Before I met Marc di Gregorio, I used to wonder how he could end up with a different woman on his arm every week. Yes, he was a rich, handsome movie star, but money wasn't everything, was it? Looks would fade, and fame was a pain in the arse, even he admitted that. But the moment his lips touched mine, I knew.

Marc kissed like Casanova crossed with a demon. He gripped the back of my neck with one hand, and the other squeezed my behind as a cloud of pheromones settled over me and threatened to steal the air from my lungs. Fire zipped through my veins. Although the script didn't strictly call for it, my lips parted, and the crew faded away as his tongue slipped into my mouth. The intensity of Richard and Alice's first kiss wasn't the only surprise. No, the sensation of Marc's A-list cock hardening against my stomach shocked the hell out of me.

"Let's keep it legal, folks," Patrick called, and when I opened my eyes, Carla was fanning herself beside him. Priscilla had a face like a thundercloud, and Feather's mouth was hanging open. Oops.

"I knew there was a reason I took this job," Marc murmured against my lips.

"Because you wanted to explore London?"

"Something like that. I'm a big fan of exploring, but I thought you were a small-town gal?"

Wait, did he mean...? He flexed his hips, and holy macaroni—he was coming on to me, the horny bastard.

"I was talking about the history and the architecture. Are you always this inappropriate?"

"Mostly, yeah."

"You know there was a whole movement about harassment in the acting industry? Lawsuits, op-eds, the works."

"If you're feeling harassed, you might want to consider taking your hand off my ass."

Dammit! I let go as if I'd been burned.

"Sorry."

"For the record, that wasn't an objection."

Patrick cleared his throat. "This is great method acting, but we need to rehearse the next scene."

Which was Priscilla's scene, not mine, but Marc kept his arm around my waist for a beat longer.

"To be continued," he whispered, too quietly for anyone but me to hear.

My jelly legs threatened to give way when he let go, then the heat turned frosty, and not only because of the ice picks shooting from Priscilla's eyes. No, it was Owen who dumped the bucket of cold water over me. Not literally, because he'd never do that, but he'd sent me a message earlier, and the memory of it had the same effect.

Just one line.

How are you?

I still hadn't replied. What on earth was I meant to say?

Oh, I'm great! Apart from the fact that I found a

cockroach in the shower this morning, and I'm eighty percent certain the guy in the flat next door is a drug dealer. Also, I have this weird love-hate thing going on with my co-star, who's definitely an arsehole but also really hot. And my other co-star hates me. So does my overdraft. I've barely slept in a week, and I'm terrified of screwing up in front of a live audience.

"You're in the way," Priscilla told me.

Story of my life.

"Sorry."

"And there's no need for tongues. We're in a play, not an adult movie."

"I didn't realise there were rules."

"That's because you're not a serious actress. What theatre experience do you have? Just a few bit parts in regional productions?"

My palm itched to slap her, and maybe I would have if I hadn't noticed Patrick's sly grin as he watched us bickering. Many, many times, I'd wondered why he'd picked me to play Alice, but suddenly it all made sense. Life imitated art. Priscilla and Eliza were both bitchy and serious, and whether she wanted Richard or not wasn't important. What *was* important? She didn't want *me* to have him. And there was a spark between Marc and me, just as there was an instant attraction between Richard and Alice.

Awkward.

I didn't want to like Marc. And I wasn't even sure I did like him, not his personality anyway. But my body responded to his in a way I couldn't control. That terrified me.

I didn't do flings.

I definitely didn't do flings with colleagues.

And I absolutely definitely didn't do flings with A-list colleagues in the midst of a sex-tape scandal.

But hot damn, Viola was right. Marc di Gregorio was

hung. Videos could be faked, but I'd felt the evidence for myself.

Carla offered me her paper fan. "Here, you look as if you need this more than I do."

"It's that obvious?"

"When I first discussed this project with Patrick and read the script, I thought there was a twenty-five percent chance that the audience would pick Alice over Eliza, but I'm flipping that on its head. Too bad there's no reliable way to quantify personality."

How was I supposed to respond to that?

I'm sorry I made Marc hard; I didn't mean to.

"Uh, will that have a negative impact on your study?"

"No, because the study is about relativity. Same actors, different audience demographics. But from a professional standpoint, I find the personality aspect fascinating." She gave me a sideways glance. "Both on and off stage."

"I feel as if I'm in a goldfish bowl," I admitted.

"At times like this, it's important to stay grounded. Keep talking to your family and friends. Don't get caught up in a world that's not real."

Carla's words hit a nerve. I didn't have many friends, only Viola really, and I wasn't going to disturb Liam and Marissa while they were on holiday. My youngest brother, Heath, still had six months left in the army—unless he decided to reenlist—which left my parents. My dad didn't talk much at all, and if I called Mum, I'd never get off the phone. The two of them were planning to drive up from Devon to watch me in the final show, and I'd have to beg Marc not to get quite so heated or she'd start dropping hints about wedding bells. My mum was convinced that everyone was destined to have a happy ending, that there was a soulmate waiting in the wings, but I didn't share her optimism. In fact, sometimes her cheerfulness made me want to jump off a cliff.

"I'll try to stay grounded," I promised Carla.

Maybe that was why I pulled out my phone and messaged Owen. The old friend my heart had never forgotten.

Me: I'm good, thanks! In London, rehearsing for a play. How are you?

I figured he'd take a few hours to reply, but the message came almost immediately.

Owen Cadwallader: Also in London working. How are the rehearsals going?

He was in London? My emotions were all over the place this week, but the weird mix of nerves and relief was new. Owen was close. Not close enough to touch, but just knowing he was in the same city gave me a strange sense of comfort.

Me: Intense. We've got less than two weeks until opening night, so we're here from dawn till dusk. What do you do now? Are your plans for world domination working out?

It was an old joke between us. Owen had been the genius who wanted to change the world—for good, obviously—while I'd offered to be his glamorous sidekick as long as I got a badass costume.

Owen Cadwallader: I head up the operations team for the UK arm of a software company. Plans for world domination are currently on hold, but we do keep a lot of data safe.

Me: Software? I could have done with you three months ago when I clicked on a link to upgrade my laptop browser and ended up with three thousand ads for Viagra.

Owen Cadwallader: Did you take it to a specialist?

Me: No, I turned it off and put it in a drawer.

And it had been languishing there ever since, just one more thing I didn't have the energy to deal with.

Owen Cadwallader: Want me to take a look?

What?

Could it really be that easy? We hadn't spoken in eight years, and although a day hadn't passed without me thinking about him, I'd been too nervous to get in touch. Now he was acting as if everything were normal between us? As if our first sort-of-date hadn't ended in disaster? As if I hadn't been carted off crying in handcuffs?

No, it couldn't be that easy. The stars never aligned that way for me.

Me: If you're willing, I could courier it to you? I'd be happy to pay for your time.

Nothing.

No response.

I stared at the phone for ten whole minutes, willing a notification to pop up, but the screen remained stubbornly blank.

And then it was time to go and kiss Marc di Gregorio again.

Six

"OMG! Tell me he's a good kisser?"

Viola's perkiness physically pained me at six o'clock in the morning, especially when I'd had no sleep.

"Who?"

"How many men have you been kissing?"

"Only one," I mumbled. "And in a purely professional capacity."

"Doesn't look that professional to me."

"Huh?"

"There are pictures, babes. Everywhere."

I scrabbled for my iPad and quickly found Viola wasn't kidding. Marc and I were front and centre on every gossip site, locked in a passionate clinch. The images had been cropped so the rest of the cast and crew weren't visible.

"Someone leaked photos from yesterday's rehearsal."

"Oh, people always do that. But still, they're *hawt*."

"Nobody leaked pictures from *Whispers in Willowbrook*."

"None of the actors in *Whispers* look like Marc di

Gregorio. Are the rumours true? I heard he often gets jiggy with his co-stars."

"Viola!"

"What?"

"He's been perfectly pleasant."

"But?" she prodded.

"But what?"

"I sense a 'but' coming."

"But... I'm confused."

"Confused how?"

"There's chemistry, everyone tells us there's chemistry, and I think I even felt it. But then Owen messaged me, and it was as if someone had dunked me in a vat of ice."

"Owen?"

"Owen who used to live next door."

"Ohmigosh! Owen the geek who sent a solicitor to rescue you from jail?"

"I prefer to think of him as Owen who saved me from failing GCSE maths. Or Owen who used to bring me gummy bears whenever I felt miserable."

Owen who "borrowed" his dad's car to pick me up from school when it was raining so I wouldn't have to walk. Owen who fell out of a tree trying to sneak into my bedroom with ice cream when I was grounded. Owen who waded through mud to rescue my boot after the laces came undone. Owen who gave me piggybacks home from the pub —the pub we weren't supposed to be in—when my feet got tired.

We'd been friends, good friends, maybe even best friends, but there had always been a cloud hanging over us. Yes, he'd lived next door in the village of Fairoaks, but we weren't equals. His family owned a beautifully restored farmhouse, while my family squashed into one of the old farm cottages. I'd scraped into Fairoaks Grammar by the skin of my teeth, and he was in the top set for everything. His parents thought I was a bad influence. Which was probably true.

"Gummy bears? Aw, that's so sweet. What did he say? Are you going to see him?"

"No, but he did offer to take a look at my duff laptop, which is great, isn't it? I said I'd courier it to him. You know, after I get back home."

"I'm sorry, what?"

"He does some kind of software stuff now. Figures. I mean, he was always into computers at school."

"You're a bloody idiot."

"Huh?"

"You're going to *courier your laptop*?"

"Yes?"

He'd eventually replied yesterday, five minutes before midnight, and he'd sent me his office address. HC Systems in Hertfordshire. I'd googled the place, and it was just a brick-and-glass building on an industrial estate, nothing like Scaramanga's island lair.

"Serena, you might not be able to see me right now, but you should know that I'm smacking my forehead. I should be smacking yours."

"What? Why?"

"He offered to fix your laptop so you would bring it to him. *Personally.* Sheesh, if you took GSCE how-to-understand-dudes, you'd get a big fat F."

"But...but...why would he suddenly want to see me? He's avoided me for years."

"It takes two to tango. You've avoided him too."

"Only because he ignored me first. I sent that message, remember?" The day after I got released from jail, I hadn't felt up to speaking, but I'd typed out a long, heartfelt text saying how sorry I was that he'd got covered in what turned out to be a mixture of red paint and pig blood. Libby's dad had owned the local butcher's shop. "He never replied."

"So maybe he just needed time to cool off."

"Eight years?"

"Message him back and say you'll deliver the laptop personally."

"Are you sure?"

"Trust me."

"Last time I trusted you, I ended up singing 'Copacabana' on stage with a bunch of drag queens."

"The drag queens were awesome. Come on, admit it. You had a great time."

"I didn't have a great hangover."

"Just message Owen, and make sure you give him your number." Viola giggled, and I heard another voice in the background. "I gotta go."

"Do you have a guy with you?"

"Serena, meet Trent. Trent, meet Serena."

A deep voice mumbled, "Hi."

"Uh, hello."

Then Viola came back. "Go hook up with at least one of your admirers, babes. It's been too long."

Ugh, this was yet another new part of the "fame" experience. Tonight, I'd been followed home, or rather, back to the horror of a flat above the kebab shop. Embarrassment warred with irritation, and embarrassment won. Tomorrow, the internet would be full of pictures of me fighting with the temperamental door lock while two barely clothed women staggered past, singing "Show Me the Way to Amarillo." On the plus side, I was less likely to get mugged if there were half a dozen witnesses with cameras watching my every move, and whatever rubbish they wrote might go some way to dispelling the notion that all actors were millionaires. The majority of us rejoiced if we found a lost penny on the pavement.

I'd been thinking about Viola's advice the whole day, and I'd spent the Tube ride writing a message, erasing it, and then writing it again.

Finally, I'd hit "send."

Me: I could actually bring the laptop to you myself—I have a few days off after the play finishes. Maybe I could buy you a coffee as a thank you?

Then I'd regretted it.

But I couldn't undo what I'd done. As I was searching for the "delete" button, I saw the three dots of doom. Owen had read the message, and he was typing a reply. But no reply came.

Why did men have to be so freaking confusing? I couldn't stand Priscilla, but at least she was straightforward in her bitchiness. Between Owen's overly polite messages, Marc's innuendos, and Patrick's constant orders of "again, but this time with more feeling," I'd had enough of Y chromosomes.

The paparazzi had followed me around Sainsbury's while I picked out a microwaveable chicken katsu curry and a chocolate eclair—cue a story about problems with my weight—and now I approached the microwave with trepidation. Every time I used it, there was an alarming buzzing noise, but when I'd tried turning on the cooker, the smell of gas had made me turn it right back off again. Yes, I'd tried reporting the issue to the landlord, but the landlord must have taken lessons from Owen because he hadn't bothered to reply.

And suddenly, the microwave wasn't a problem anymore. A *bang*, a couple of sparks, and it stopped working entirely. Fantastic. Now I had lukewarm curry, and wasn't rice a bit dodgy when it wasn't cooked through? I didn't have time for food poisoning. I was in the middle of googling the dangers of *Bacillus cereus* when my phone rang.

Owen calling.

Like, an actual phone call, not via social media.

What the heck? He still had my number? I dropped the phone into the katsu curry, then cursed because was anything else going to go wrong in my life this month?

The ringing stopped.

Without thinking things through, I stuck my finger in the sauce and called back.

"I'm here, I'm here. Just a minute... The phone's swimming in curry, and I can't find the paper towel."

Owen's soft chuckle made my heart skip. I'd missed that. I'd missed *him*.

"I thought you might be busy."

"If you count blowing up the microwave as busy, then yes, I am."

"Blowing up the microwave? You're still the same old Serena."

"Hey, less of the 'old.' And I have changed. I almost never eat ice cream for dinner anymore, although now I'm regretting that because at least ice cream doesn't require cooking." Finally, I found a handful of napkins and wiped the worst of the sauce away. "Is it safe to eat rice if it isn't completely hot?"

"That depends on how it's been stored."

"It was in a fridge. I just bought it from the supermarket half an hour ago."

"Then it should be fine."

Eight years, and we were talking about rice, but I'd take it.

"Have you already had dinner?" I asked.

"An hour ago." A long pause. "I spent all evening trying to decide whether I should call or not. I wasn't sure you'd answer. It's been so long since we've spoken."

"I'll always answer, but I left the ball in your court. I just figured it was you who didn't want to talk."

"What do you mean, the ball was in my court?"

"The message I sent... You never replied."

"What message?"

"After I..." I sucked in a breath. "After I got out of jail. The apology I sent. I know it was just a text message, but honestly, I couldn't stop crying enough to speak, and then you went back to Cambridge without another word."

"I didn't get a text message."

"But it said it had been delivered."

I hadn't been imagining that; I'd checked the screen a hundred times and even googled "Can a message say it's been delivered when it really hasn't been?"

"I didn't get a message," he repeated. "Mum told me your mother called her and said you needed some space, so I gave you that."

"I... What?"

"I kept thinking you'd call when you were ready, but then you never did."

"My mum didn't call your mum. At least, I don't think she did. Why would she have done that? She told me I should pull myself together and get out of bed."

And when I'd mumbled an excuse and burrowed under

the duvet, she'd told me the linen needed washing, rolled me over, and stolen the sheets.

"Then I don't under—" Another pause. "Ah, fuck." The tinkling sound of breaking glass came through the phone, followed by barking. "Fuck, fuck, fuck."

"What? What happened? Are you okay?"

"I'll call you back."

Seven

Ten minutes passed. Twenty. I scraped the curry into the bin because my appetite had deserted me and then returned to pacing. The couple next door—not the drug dealer side, the other side—were having an argument, and the guy upstairs had left his TV on so loud that I could hear every word. I tried banging on the ceiling with a shoe, but he didn't take the hint.

Should I send Owen a message? Say I was sorry again? Had I come across too accusatory? Yes, I'd pointed out the text message issue, but he *had* ignored me. Or I could call him back, but what if it was a bad moment? Maybe he had a girlfriend, or worse, a wife, and she'd overheard him on the phone? Our conversation had been innocuous, but my feelings weren't, and I didn't want to be the other woman.

I should just go to bed. Yes, that was the best idea. I needed sleep, although I wouldn't get any; I was certain of that.

The phone rang.

I dived for it.

"Owen?"

"Serena."

"Are you okay?"

"Am I okay? No. No, I'm not okay."

"Should I go?"

"No." He sure was fond of his pauses, wasn't he? "It's safe to say that whatever shaky relationship I still had left with my mother is now over. Serena, I'm the one who needs to apologise. For being too stubborn to get in touch, and for not seeing how manipulative my mother could be."

"Huh?"

"I just called her. She admitted that she deleted your message, and she also made up the call from your mum."

"But why? Why would she..." I trailed off because I realised I already knew the answer. "She thought I wasn't good enough to be friends with you, didn't she? I guess I always knew that, deep down, but—"

"She was wrong."

"I thought you'd decided on a clean break. That you'd outgrown our friendship. We didn't talk so much after you went to uni, and we were going in two different directions."

"I had a heavy workload, that's all. Our chats were something I always looked forward to, but I should have made more time for you." Then, more quietly, "I thought you were angry I didn't prevent what happened that day. I saw them coming with the bucket, and there was a split second when I could have stopped the drenching, but it just didn't click what they were doing."

"I never blamed you. In fact, I still owe you a new tuxedo."

"Forget it."

So much time wasted. I never had liked Mrs. Cadwallader, but I hadn't realised the animosity ran deep enough that she'd lie to her own son just to stop him from seeing me.

"Where do we go from here?" I whispered.

"Where do you want to go?"

"For coffee? I'll be done with this play in five weeks, and then I'll basically be unemployed, so I'll have all the time in the world."

"I'll put the kettle on. Unless you fancy getting a late dinner after your play two weeks from Friday?"

"Why? Will you be in London again?"

"I've got a ticket."

Owen was coming to watch *The Other Woman*? Suddenly, the idea of kissing Marc in front of an audience felt a hundred times more daunting. Bad enough that my parents were coming to see the play, without the man I'd spent half a lifetime hiding my feelings from showing up to watch me snogging a guy who wasn't him.

Please, let the audience vote for Priscilla two weeks from Friday.

But I didn't say any of that, of course.

"A late dinner sounds great, but I won't be done until eleven. I doubt anywhere will still be serving food at that time."

"I'll find somewhere and book a table."

Really?

Two weeks. Two weeks until I could see Owen again. Never in my life had I wished so hard that time travel was a thing.

"Okay! It's a date!" Crap. "Uh, not a *date* date obviously, but it'll be good to see you. I mean, it's been so long. How have you been? Did you get a dog? I heard one barking earlier."

"His name is Moose."

"Moose? You called your dog Moose?"

"He came with the name. The shelter said it was the only thing he had that was his, so I kept it."

Wow. That was so...so domesticated. I struggled to keep the spider plant in my bathroom alive. It didn't seem to like the new digs any more than I did, and over the past week, it had begun looking decidedly brown.

"Where do you live now? I know your parents moved away soon after the, uh, incident."

"They're in Cheshire. I bought a place near Broxbourne."

"Broxbourne? I don't even know where that is."

"Hertfordshire." Near his office. That made sense. I couldn't think straight this evening. "How about you?"

"No pets, just a plant. I did have two plants, but the cactus died. And I've lived all over the place, but mostly back in the Cotswolds for the past three years because that's where *Whispers in Willowbrook* is filmed."

"Tell me they're not planning to kill off Detective Cartwright?"

"You watch the show?"

"Every episode. They'd be crazy not to bring you back."

"They haven't told me yet, but I think they might not. I had a bit of a falling-out with a wardrobe assistant." I buried my head in my hands. Owen was the first person I'd told about my recent faux pas, and I definitely didn't want to dump my problems on him, but we always used to talk about everything. "She was picking on an intern, and I told her that wasn't cool, but it turned out she was the producer's daughter. I know she's been complaining behind my back."

"And the producer has the final say?"

"Exactly."

"Things have a way of working out. Aren't you spending time with a Hollywood guy now?"

"Marc?"

"The two of you are all over social media." Owen

sounded roughly as thrilled as I felt about the situation. "Doesn't name recognition help in the acting industry?"

"I guess." My agent *had* emailed this morning to see if I'd be interested in fronting a new brand of lipstick, plus I might be able to pick up more audiobook work. "Hopefully I'll get some offers, assuming I survive the play, that is."

"Things aren't going well?"

"The schedule is intense, and if Libby Sieber wasn't an only child, I'd suspect Priscilla Prentice was her older sister."

"Priscilla Prentice—she's your co-star?"

"That's right."

"Is she giving you trouble?"

"Not in a 'let's ruin prom' kind of way, but I wouldn't exactly call us friends. The casting's perfect, though. Enemies in life, enemies in art."

"That doesn't sound like a comfortable working environment."

"It's only for five more weeks, and I've had worse."

"Worse? Where?"

"So, before I landed the part on *Whispers in Willowbrook*, I worked in a restaurant for a while, and the owner was an absolute creep. Oh, sure, his hand just kept accidentally landing on my backside, and the camera in the bathroom just installed itself."

"He put a *camera in the bathroom*?"

Owen's voice was tight, and I'd never heard him sound quite so pissed before. Perhaps I shouldn't have mentioned that little snippet? I didn't want to scare him off again by being the awkward girl with all the issues.

"He didn't hide it very well, so I noticed straight away and flushed it."

And then he fired me because I "wasn't a team player."

"Which restaurant was it?"

"Oh, not one you'd know. I was living in Manchester at the time."

"I'm going to need a name, Serena." A pause. I heard Owen take a deep breath. "Just in case I'm ever there on business. I need to know where to avoid."

"Uh, it was called Mega Munch. Not a place you'd go to, I shouldn't think, especially if you're with clients. And the hygiene sucked. You know why I spotted the camera? Because it was in a soap dispenser, and I was so flabbergasted to see an actual cleaning product that I tried using it right away, and the pump didn't work. Anyhow, I found a better side hustle, so no more serving burgers for me."

"What's the better side hustle?"

"I narrate audiobooks. Under a pseudonym so far, but I'm considering using my own name. I mean, now that more people know it."

"What's your pseudonym?"

Probably I shouldn't have started down this road. "Oh, they're not your sort of books." Smut. The books I read as Susie Valentine were pure smut. *Change the subject, idiot.* "Tell me more about what you've been up to... Is Moose your only pet?"

"I know what you're trying to do."

"Huh?"

"You're too self-deprecating for your own good. Serena, you're a talented actress. Don't put yourself down."

Where else had I heard that already this week? *Be a queen.* I'd consider putting on a crown tomorrow, but for tonight, I could do without Owen listening to me gush over another man's eggplant, even if that man was fictional. Hell, one of Susie Valentine's masterpieces even came with tentacles.

"I'm too tired to hold myself up tonight. Maybe in the morning."

As I'd hoped he would, Owen just laughed. It was the best sound in the world. "I'll give you a temporary pass." Phew. "Moose is my only pet, technically."

"Technically?"

"There's also Simon the squirrel. Who I'm beginning to suspect might actually be Simone after the camera caught some highly inappropriate behaviour on my bedroom windowsill two weeks ago."

"Why were you filming your bedroom windowsill?"

"He—she—built a nest there. I told a few of the guys at work, and it snowballed. I'll send you the link. Wait a second..."

It snowballed? I clicked on the link and found Owen wasn't kidding. Simone the squirrel not only had a nest, she had a picnic table, a tiny rug, a clawfoot tub filled with what looked like dirt, a champagne saucer filled with water, and even a framed portrait stuck to the brickwork. According to the view counter in the corner, there were seventy-nine other people watching the plump squirrel get some shut-eye, and she even had her own website. I tried to squint at the garden beyond, but it was too dark to see much.

"Don't worry, the champagne glass is actually made from plastic, and I glued it down."

"Who painted the picture?"

"Janice in accounts."

"Your squirrel has better furniture than I do."

"You want me to buy you a new dining set?" he joked.

I didn't fancy admitting that I had no dining table at all, only a coffee table and a cushion, so I forced a laugh. Then I fell asleep listening to Owen telling me about Moose's fondness for collecting socks, even if someone happened to be wearing them at the time. Moose had a whole collection of stolen footwear, apparently—Owen had found it hidden in the stair cupboard when he was hunting for a pair of boots.

That night, I didn't dream about blood or interns or Marc. It was my first good night of rest since leaving the Cotswolds.

Eight

"Did you watch Soreen's tape?"

"Uh..."

Marc offered a takeaway cup with my name written on the side. "I only ask because you haven't been able to look me in the eye today."

I'd tried to avoid it, honestly I had, and I'd been successful for almost a week. But when I was aimlessly scrolling through social media on the loo earlier, it had been right there. I mean, it just started playing. I hadn't clicked a button or anything. And now I had to try and act normal around a man who knew exactly how to use his generously sized cock. I took a deep breath and then swallowed a sip of coffee. We were on a break while Priscilla had her costume adjusted, a welcome respite, or so I'd thought.

Breathe, Serena. In and out.

"You did," Marc said, with too much confidence for my liking. "Nobody can fake a blush like that one without help from a good make-up artist."

"Maybe just a brief clip? I'm so sorry. Uh, I think my

settings got messed up, and...and... I realise it was totally unprofessional."

I'd only been trying to distract myself. After I'd sent Owen a "Good morning!" text and checked in on Squirrel Cam, I'd grown antsy waiting for a reply. Was Owen still a night owl? Back in our school days, he'd hated mornings.

"Chill, sweetheart. Do I look upset?"

"I still can't believe you're being so blasé about the whole thing."

"Yeah, I'd rather it hadn't gone public, but it doesn't exactly show me in a bad light. Have you seen celebgossip.com? I believe the words 'considerate lover' were mentioned, plus I'm getting the sympathy vote."

It was true; the media had sided with Marc over Soreen, unusual in this age of #MeToo. I needed a publicist like Jessica. She'd played it perfectly, with compassion and concern and a general railing against poor moderation policies on social media. Marc had been careful not to target his ex. Soreen, on the other hand, had been whining twenty-four-seven in every medium possible.

"Even so..." I shuddered. "I can't think of anything worse than the world seeing my naked backside. Soreen must have no shame whatsoever."

"My agent heard a rumour that she's trying to get into adult movies, so I guess she thought of it as an audition."

"That's so...so brazen. I'd never dare to behave like that."

"I know, sweetheart. You're a good girl." Marc leaned in closer, and goosebumps popped up on my arms. "So if you feel like checking out the goods in the flesh, just let me know."

I choked on my coffee. Marc di Gregorio was hitting on me? Blatantly hitting on me? Colombia's finest came out of my nose and dribbled down my shirt, which ought to have put him off if nothing else did. My mind spun—in the space of a week, I'd gone from living as a crazy cat woman without the cats to reconnecting with my teenage crush to being propositioned by number three on *Imagine* magazine's list of the world's most eligible bachelors. Was I being punk'd?

"Careful," Marc warned. "I don't know that Heimlich thing."

"Then don't offer to show me your twig and berries while I'm drinking. Seriously? Does that line ever work?"

"I have a surprisingly high success rate."

That actually wasn't a surprise at all. "I hate to break it to you, but the fact that women are willing to hop into bed with you might be something to do with your pretty face and not your gift of the gab."

"C'mon, we have chemistry. You feel it, don't you? Every time I kiss you, your nipples harden."

Rats, he'd noticed? "That's just a physical reaction."

"You're single, I'm single, and I'm in London for five more weeks. Think about it."

"So you're offering...what? Five weeks of sex? Nothing more?"

"No strings. I find it's better to be upfront, and I make a terrible boyfriend."

"Why?"

"Why is it better to be upfront?"

"No, why do you make a terrible boyfriend?"

He ticked off the points on his fingers. "I'm self-centred, I'm too career-focused, and I have issues with commitment."

"Have you considered seeing a therapist?"

"I already tried that."

"How did it go?"

"I had to hire a professional cleaning crew to get the cum stains off her couch."

Oh. My. Goodness.

"I... I don't even know what to say to that. I guess, have you considered seeing a *male* therapist?"

"Nah, sweetheart. I'm straight."

"I meant for actual therapy."

"Like, talking?"

"Exactly."

"Talking's overrated." Marc trailed a finger up my arm. "So, what do you think? Feel like experimenting with sin for a few weeks? I have a great hotel suite. A king-sized bed, room service, a jacuzzi..."

Room service and a jacuzzi? Oh my... A week ago, perhaps I'd have thrown caution to the wind and taken him up on the offer. I mean, he was Marc di Gregorio—Marc *freaking* di Gregorio—and everyone thought we were sleeping together anyway. And I did actually kind of like him. Yes, he was a filthy commitment-phobe, but he wasn't making any false promises. He'd set a deadline, and I already knew from Soreen's moans of pleasure that his abilities in the bedroom absolutely matched his ego.

But a lot had happened in a week.

My world had tilted on its axis.

And if by hooking up with Marc, I destroyed the fragile relationship I was rebuilding with Owen, I'd never forgive myself.

I still loved Owen, as a friend and maybe more. I always would.

"Sorry, but I can't. It's not you, it's me."

"That's usually my line."

"There's...there's somebody else."

"Weren't you single this time last week? Or did the gossip magazines get that wrong?"

"It's complicated. We're not exactly together, but I think someday I want to be."

Marc watched me carefully for several moments, and

then his expression softened. He wasn't acting now. At least, I didn't think he was.

"Then he's a lucky guy."

"You're not upset?"

"Nah, sweetheart. Disappointed? Yeah, because you're hotter than Death Valley in July, but I'm not gonna be the other man."

"Thank you."

He brought the back of my hand to his lips. "Friends?"

"Friends. Uh, he's coming to see the play next Friday, so do you think we could avoid using tongues that night?"

"You don't want to make him jealous?"

"No, I— Wait, do you think that would help?"

"If I was taking the softly, softly approach and I saw another man kissing my girl, I'd go full caveman."

Hmm. I hadn't considered that possibility. But what if Owen backed right off because he didn't want to compete with Mr. Hollywood?

"Can I let you know?"

"Sure, sweetheart. Finish what's left of your coffee, and let's get back to work."

I survived the week.

I survived Marc's endless innuendos, although I had to respect him for never overstepping. He'd left the next move up to me, and he didn't cross the line. Did I? I got tempted once or twice, but my nightly calls with Owen kept me grounded. We talked into the early hours and filled in some of the missing parts of our lives, although he avoided getting too personal. There was a distance that hadn't been there eight years ago. I hoped that in time the gap would close, but I was grateful for what we had right now.

Priscilla didn't get any less bitchy, but even Patrick's patience seemed to be wearing thin. I overheard him complaining to Carla, and Carla's off-the-record opinion was that Priscilla was a narcissist.

Four weeks to go.

Feather kept me supplied with coffee, and Owen delivered half a dozen bags of gummy bears to the theatre, which made my heart flutter. Simone grew decidedly fatter. Janice—she who'd painted the portrait—had sent a care package full of hazelnuts and sunflower seeds, and Owen refilled the picnic table every morning.

The next week promised to be challenging for both of us. I had the fanfare of opening night, endless media "opportunities," and performances every evening, while Owen was negotiating a multimillion-pound contract in Peterborough and overseeing a new product launch. The company he worked for was involved with network security and data protection and a whole bunch of other stuff I didn't understand. Ever since his boss had expanded the company into the US, married an American, and practically moved to Virginia, Owen had been promoted to a senior managerial position. Which left me slightly in awe. He'd graduated university with honours and landed a well-respected job, while I pretended to trip over dead bodies for a living and got pictured in the tabloids with mustard on my top.

In six days, I'd see Owen in person. Would he still look the same? As well as Piper, his old classmates had called him Beanpole because he'd never quite grown into his height, or sometimes SpongeBob because he wore thick-rimmed glasses like the cartoon character. Or Shaggy, because he'd always found a hundred things more important to do than visiting the barber. He'd shrugged off the insults, but I knew that under the brave face, he'd been hurt by the spite. Anyhow, the glasses were cool now, and his "Pi - 3.14 times better than cookies" T-shirt would probably go down quite well with his new colleagues.

Six more days, and he'd promised to call me every evening.

I just had to survive the critics' reviews, the dodgy wiring in my flat, and a night-time photoshoot on the roof terrace at the fancy hotel Marc and Patrick were staying in. Someone would have to airbrush the dark smudges from under my eyes.

Six days...

Nine

Oh, hell no.

I already had a headache from Priscilla, but at the sight of the water dribbling through my living room ceiling, the niggle turned into full-on pounding. Had a pipe burst? The carpet squelched underfoot as I stepped forward to take a closer look.

"Just my freaking luck," I muttered.

The play opened tomorrow. Tonight of all nights, I needed sleep, but as I stood staring in horror at the small lake that was forming around the sofa, a chunk of plaster fell down and narrowly missed my foot. Shit! I needed to call the landlord.

Who of course didn't answer.

I left a message explaining the situation, but where the heck was I meant to sleep? I didn't trust the wiring when it was dry, let alone when it was dripping, and what if the place burned down in the early hours? Was there a stopcock somewhere? I found a tap under the kitchen sink and closed it, but the water kept on gushing. Was it even coming from my pipes? What if the problem was in the apartment above?

I traipsed up the stairs and banged on the door, but nobody answered. Honestly, I felt like crying, but the floor was quite damp enough already.

Should I call a plumber? What choice did I have? I'd paid up front for the whole two-month rental, so the chances of me getting the money back were negligible, but if I waited much longer for the landlord to return my call, I'd need a dinghy instead of a bed.

My phone rang. I'd been looking forward to Owen's call all day, but now I had to deal with...with this.

"Can I call you back?" I asked.

"What's the problem?"

"How do you know there's a problem?"

"Because I know you, Serena. I can hear the worry in your voice. What can I do to help?"

"Do you know a good plumber?"

"A plumber?"

"There's a water leak. In the ceiling. The landlord's on radio silence, my upstairs neighbour isn't answering the door, and I really, really wish I had my wellies with me." The tears came. I couldn't stop them. "I just want to go home. This was meant to be the role of a lifetime, and all I want to do is hightail it back to the Cotswolds."

"It'll be okay, I promise. Give me your address and five minutes."

He only needed two. Owen rang back while I was setting cereal bowls under the torrent in an attempt to stem the damage—a pointless exercise because I couldn't empty them fast enough.

"Someone will be with you in the next twenty minutes," he said.

"A plumber?"

"No, but they'll assess the situation and do whatever needs to be done. Just pack your things."

"I don't have anywhere else to go."

"You're not staying in a damp flat."

"But—"

"Let me do the worrying tonight, Serena. The people coming are from Blackwood Security, and they'll be carrying identification. Let me know when they arrive, okay?"

Blackwood Security? I didn't need protection; I needed an umbrella. But if one of them knew how to shut the water off, I'd kiss their feet. And Owen's. Hell, I'd kiss his feet anyway. Not that I had a foot fetish or anything. Yes, okay, I'd sold a few pictures of my feet online when I was at theatre school, but I'd been strapped for cash and short of rent money.

Even though I was expecting it, the knock on the door still made me jump. I cracked it open and found two black-clad men staring back at me.

"Ms. Carlisle?"

"Are you the security people?"

"That's right. I'm Nye, and this is Zander." They held out official-looking ID cards. Both could have given Marc a run for his money in the looks department, but they had a hardness about them that Mr. Hollywood was missing. "I gather you've got a plumbing problem?"

I opened the door wider so they could step inside, and Nye sucked in a breath when he saw the waterfall coming from the ceiling. Until today, I'd always found the sound of running water relaxing, but now I was having a rethink.

"It's getting worse," I said. "It was more of a trickle when I got home."

"Yikes," Nye said. "Yes, I see why Owen called us."

"Do you do plumbing as well as security?"

"We solve problems."

Zander peered up at the hole. "Do you know the layout of the apartment upstairs?"

"I've never been in there, and my neighbour isn't home. Or at least, he's not answering the door."

"We'll take a look." He offered a charming smile. "Just relax, and we'll get this all sorted out."

Two hours later, I huddled on a concrete bench outside the kebab shop. A paramedic had given me a blanket, and I pulled it tighter around my shoulders as I waited for yet another detective to question me. Crime scene tape flapped in the stiff breeze.

"Want another cuppa, love?" a police officer asked.

"I just want to go to bed."

"Won't be long now."

"Why do I have to stay here? I keep telling you, I didn't see anything. I wasn't even here all day."

"I'm afraid we have to follow procedure, ma'am."

On the plus side, the water had been turned off. On the minus side, when Nye and Zander checked out my upstairs neighbour's flat—the door had been unlocked, apparently —they'd found him floating lifeless in the bath, the taps still turned on full. Now crime scene investigators were traipsing in and out, and even if there hadn't been a flood in my flat, I wouldn't have been allowed back inside anyway. The landlord had finally shown up. Needless to say, he wasn't thrilled about the situation, and the way he grumbled, you'd think it was all my fault.

Nye said that accommodation tonight wouldn't be a problem, but he'd been worryingly vague when it came to the details. Thank goodness Owen had told me to pack. I'd managed to grab my suitcase before we were kicked out of the building, so at least I had clean underwear.

My phone rang. Why was Marc still awake?

"What's going on, sweetheart?"

"Huh?"

"With the cops?"

"How do you know there are cops?"

"It's all over Facebook. Feather saw the news and texted Patrick, and he called me. There are pictures everywhere."

Of course there were. I raised my weary head as some nosy ghoul snapped another photo on his camera phone. The reporters were here in droves too, although a pair of constables who didn't look old enough to wear a uniform had kept the press outside the cordon.

"Brilliant."

"What happened? Are you okay?"

"Oh, they just found a dead body in the flat above mine. Plus my living room is flooded and part of the ceiling fell down."

"Are you shitting me? And they've left you sitting there on a bench?"

"It's procedure. One more interview and then I can leave, apparently."

"Do you have somewhere to stay?"

"I don't know. I don't know anything."

"I have a two-bedroom suite. Want me to send a car? Just tell me where you are."

Did I? The idea of curling up under a duvet in a fancy hotel room made me weep with relief, but would that lead to awkwardness between Marc and me? After I'd turned down his advances, I definitely didn't want to give him the wrong idea.

"Maybe? I—"

A shadow fell over me. I looked up to find Nye and a man who seemed vaguely familiar, but I couldn't quite place him. Tall, dark, and handsome. Short brown hair with a hint of curl. A neatly trimmed beard. Dimples. A tight T-shirt that stretched over well-defined pecs. Worried brown eyes.

No...

No, it couldn't be...

The T-shirt said "I closed my laptop to be here."

"Serena."

One word, and my heart puddled in my chest. "Owen? What the...? You look, uh..."

Incendiary.

He glanced down at himself. "I started going to the gym."

"Where are your glasses?"

"I got LASIK."

When he smiled, I saw that he'd had his teeth straightened as well. Holy hotness. All these years, I'd been fantasising about a slightly older version of the skinny nerd I'd adored as a teen, and now Superman's younger brother was standing in front of me?

"You look good. Uh, healthy. I meant healthy. Owen, what are you doing here? I thought you were in Peterborough?"

"When I realised you were in trouble, I got into the car and started driving." He tucked a lock of hair behind my ear. "This wasn't quite how I'd imagined seeing you again, but I'll take it."

A sob burst out of me, followed by another and another, and then I was wrapped up in Owen's arms. He gave the best hugs. Whenever teenage me had been miserable, I just used to put my head on his shoulder and wait for him to work his magic.

"Serena?" The voice was tinny. "You okay?"

Crap! I'd forgotten Marc. I pressed the phone to my ear.

"I'm fine. An old friend just showed up."

"Is this *the* old friend?"

"Uh, yes?"

He gave a soft chuckle. "Good luck, sweetheart. Don't forget to get some sleep, and I'll see you tomorrow."

"Who was that?" Owen asked.

"Marc."

"I see. Are you going to stay with him tonight?"

"He offered, but..." Boy, Owen's chest was *solid*. I leaned my cheek against his shoulder and sighed. For the first time in years, I was exactly where I wanted to be. "I missed you."

"Do you want to borrow my guest room?"

I nodded, and a tear dripped from the end of my nose. *Such a damn mess.*

"Is Serena done here?" he asked Nye.

"I'll hurry things along."

Ten

"Morning." The bed dipped as Owen sat on the edge, and the delicious aroma of hot chocolate wafted in my direction. "How are you feeling?"

I didn't remember much about the journey to Broxbourne. Owen had half carried me to his car after yet another detective asked me to go over last night's events. Unfortunately, I'd made the mistake of mentioning the drug dealer next door, which had led to a hundred more questions from the police and a lot of frowning from Owen. I was never going back to that apartment again—he'd been very clear on that.

So now I was in his guest room, which was roughly the size of the entire flat I'd just left and came with an en-suite bathroom, a chaise longue, and a small balcony. I'd only caught a few glimpses of Owen's home, but the parts I had seen were beautiful.

"I still can't believe I'm here. That you're here."

"I considered climbing up a tree and in through the window the way I always used to, but then I decided the stairs were more civilised."

"Do you remember the time you fell out of the tree?"

He rolled up his left sleeve. "I still have the scar."

Except now the scar was covered by a tattoo that went from his wrist to his shoulder.

Jumping jackdaws, I'd never been a tattoo girl, but the sight of all that ink made my thighs clench. Owen looked like a cyborg. Skin peeled back to reveal gears and pistons, cables and springs.

"I designed it myself," he explained. "Theoretically, the machinery would actually work."

"I... Wow. I guess I never imagined you with a tattoo."

"Me neither. It was my boss's idea."

"What kind of company do you work for?"

Owen chuckled. "Luke's become a good friend over the years. There was an axe-throwing contest at his wife's birthday party, and there might have been beer involved, so we ended up making a side bet."

"Alcohol and axe-throwing?"

He pulled a face. "It seemed like a good idea at the time. Anyhow, the loser had to get a tattoo."

"And he won?"

"Actually, his ex-girlfriend won overall. He only came nineteenth."

"Let me get this straight... Your boss, who I'm assuming is an intelligent man, went axe-throwing with his current wife and his ex-girlfriend? Was he not afraid someone would die?"

"It was an amicable break-up."

I must have looked dubious.

"Yes, I thought those were a myth too," Owen said. "But it's true, I swear. I went to the wedding, and his ex was a bridesmaid."

Wow. I'd run into an ex at a wedding once, and after he suggested "a quick shag for old times' sake," I'd been forced to climb out of a bathroom window. Then I nearly broke my ankle fleeing across the golf course where the reception was being held. A golfer yelled at me for getting in the way, and I almost got run over by a caddy in a cart—hardly my finest hour.

I peered more closely at Owen's arm. The tattoo was a work of art, and when I squinted, I could just make out the old half-inch scar hidden in the shadow of a gear wheel.

"You didn't consider a smaller design?"

"I did consider it."

"And then you chose this?"

"Do you like it?"

Was I shocked? Totally. I'd never pictured Owen with any tattoo, let alone such a dramatic one, but how well did I really know him now? We'd grown apart, and I hated that. Hated that I hadn't been in his life for so long. But did I like the ink? Hell yes.

"I do like it."

"My mother detests it." He sighed. "She overheard me telling someone about the bet and gave me a lecture. Axe-throwing is dangerous, tattoos are uncouth, my friends are bad influences, blah, blah, blah. 'You will not get a tattoo, Owen,'" he mimicked. "'I forbid it.'"

"Did she have a heart attack when she saw it?"

"Well, so she hasn't actually seen it yet."

"Chickenshit."

"Someone told her about it, and she yelled down the phone at me."

I giggled as I traced a cog with a finger. "I bet she did. Was it painful?"

"The yelling or the tattoo?"

"The tattoo."

I'd had firsthand experience of Mrs. Cadwallader's

shrieking, and I already knew the damage that could do to a person's eardrums.

"It was like having a sharp nail repeatedly run over my skin. The first time I got a tattoo, I was slightly inebriated, and somehow I didn't remember how bad it could be."

"You have *another* tattoo?"

"A much smaller one."

"Where? What is it?"

He smiled, but unless I was imagining it, there was a sadness in his eyes too.

"Maybe someday, I'll show you." He brushed hair away from my face, an old habit of his and one that made me shiver inside. Did he realise what those barely-there touches did to me? "What time do you have to be at work today?"

"Uh... Nine o'clock. What time is it?"

"Seven. There's a car waiting outside, and the driver will take you back to Dalston whenever you're ready."

I pushed myself up to a sitting position. "You're not coming with me?" Rats, how needy did I sound? "I mean, not that I expected you to or anything."

"I wish I could come, but I can't afford to fuck up this deal. If we land this contract, we'll be able to secure several jobs and create half a dozen more."

"You have to go back to Peterborough?"

"Only for a few days. I'll be at your play on Friday, and I can take next week off." Owen leaned down, and for a moment, I thought he was going to kiss me. *Hoped* he was going to kiss me. But he only hooked a finger under my necklace and lifted it for a closer look. My cheeks burned. "Didn't I give you this?"

"Uh, yes?"

"And you've kept it for all these years?"

"It reminded me of a time when I was happy." An

expression I couldn't read crossed his face, and I caught myself chewing my lip. New Owen could be a little intimidating. "It's fine, honestly. You go to work, and I can sort out a hotel."

"No, you can stay here. I'll give you a key. There's a direct train to Dalston from Broxbourne Station, or if you'd rather travel by car, I'll arrange for a driver to come each day."

I didn't like the idea of staying in this place alone.

Without him.

Which was irrational. And also unreasonable.

Owen had dropped everything to help me yesterday—if he hadn't stepped in, a dead body in a bath would probably have fallen into my living room in the middle of the night— and now he was offering to lend me his beautiful house. I should be grateful, not greedy. But that didn't stop me from wishing I could have him all to myself.

"You're sure you don't mind me being here on my own?"

"Make yourself at home."

"I really appreciate it. And the train will be fine. My budget doesn't stretch to taxis at the moment."

"I wasn't asking you to pay for it." He placed a key with a plastic fob attached onto the bedside table. "The alarm panel is in the hall closet. You can use the panel beside the front door to tap in and out, but if you need the code, it's zero-four-zero-three."

My chest tightened. Four-three. The fourth of March.

"That's my birthday."

"I know. And I owe you eight presents." Owen rose to his feet, and he looked so much more imposing than he used to. The geek had turned into a living god. "Serena, I have to go. Call me if you need anything, and I'll see you on Friday."

"What if I just need to chat?"

Did he know how sexy that smile was? When it hit me full force, I wanted to drag him down onto the bed with me.

"As I said, call me."

Eleven

S ometimes, I wondered why I'd stuck with acting for so many years.

Tonight, I remembered.

I remembered every line, every move, every nuance, and we received a standing ovation for our performances. Alice had won the audience over and claimed her man while Eliza fell victim to her career ambitions. The final act of the play was set on Valentine's Day—ironic when the play's run finished on the twelfth of February—and I cried real tears when Richard chased Alice across the city and confessed his love with a single red rose. What a freaking rush! Okay, so Priscilla still hated my guts, but what was new?

"Fuck, this high is better than coke," Marc said as we walked off stage.

"Which you absolutely haven't taken, right?"

He flashed me a grin. "Absolutely not."

Two days ago, I'd have swooned at that smile, but now that I'd become acquainted with Owen's fifty-shades-of-gorgeous alter ego, I was basically immune to anything Marc di Gregorio might throw at me.

"Today Dalston, tomorrow the world. Although I'd settle for the Cotswolds."

"Still haven't heard about the next season of *Whispers in Willowbrook*?"

"Not yet."

"Serena," a reporter called. "Is it true your neighbour was murdered last night?"

"Do I look like a medical examiner?" I muttered under my breath, but I recognised the woman, unfortunately. Kendra Stapleton wrote the "What's On and When" column for a big national newspaper, which meant I had to be nice to her.

Marc slung an arm around my shoulders and steered me in her direction. "That's a question for the cops, Kendra. But didn't Serena do a terrific job on stage tonight?"

The reporter smirked. "You certainly looked as if you were enjoying yourself. Are the rumours true? Are you and Serena an item?"

"A gentleman never kisses and tells."

"You're not a gentleman," I told him, and Kendra seemed to find that hilarious.

"No, but I play one in the movies."

"Are you heading back to LA next month?" she asked. "When does filming for *Trouble in Paradise* start?"

"In six weeks, but we're shooting on location in Egypt. Have you met Priscilla? Let me introduce you."

"Serena, I'm hearing whispers about *Willowbrook*. Any comment on those?"

Just like that, the elation evaporated and a cold sense of dread crept in. I still had no idea whether I'd be keeping my job or not. My agent had tried giving the producer a nudge, but he was giving her the silent treatment too.

"I'm not sure which whispers you mean."

"About Detective Cartwright—is it true she's going to be the next victim of the Moorside Menace?"

They *were* killing her off? The dread turned to full-on nausea, but Marc rescued me again.

"Are you asking her to give spoilers? Serena's a professional—she's not going to ruin the show for the fans."

And then Priscilla was there, and for once, I was grateful for her "me, me, me" attitude. She elbowed me out of the way and planted herself in front of Ms. Nosy-with-a-Notepad.

"Kendra, how lovely to see you. Are you coming back tomorrow? It's impossible to judge the play on the strength of only one of the possible endings."

I backed away quietly. Despite my protests, there was a car outside waiting for me, and all I wanted to do was hightail it back to my temporary refuge. After one glass of champagne with Marc and Patrick—champagne I wasn't in the mood to drink—I found myself on the way back to Broxbourne and a late-night catch-up with Owen.

"Swear on my life, I'm never taking another job outside the city."

Day two of *The Other Woman*, and Alice had won the vote again. The atmosphere in the theatre energised me, but by the time I reached Broxbourne, the rush had turned to exhaustion. Bone-weary tiredness. I wanted Owen, but what I got was Viola. I'd tried calling Owen, but his voicemail answered—*hi, this is Owen; when you hear the beep, hang up and send me a text message*—so now I was sitting on his sofa, drinking his wine, and wondering where the heck he was at this time of night. Yesterday evening, he'd congratulated me on a successful opening and then we'd watched two episodes of *The Big Bang Theory*, him in his hotel room and me in my borrowed bed, and we'd planned to pick up where we left off tonight. But now he'd gone AWOL.

"There's no indoor plumbing in Wyoming?"

"Barely," Viola grumbled. "A tepid shower and taps that drip constantly. And raccoons! Raccoons everywhere, and when I complained, the motel owner's wife just got out a hunting rifle."

I gasped. "She threatened you?"

"No, she shot the raccoons. *Bang, bang, bang,* and she cut off their tails and hung them up like fluffy little trophies. Now I have to live with the guilt for the rest of my life. I've gone vegetarian, by the way."

"Because of the raccoons?"

"That and I'm so, so sick of hamburgers. All I want is a salad. How are things going with the Hollywood hunk? I managed to pick up half a bar of signal the day before yesterday, and celebgossip.com said you'd absolutely, definitely hooked up with Marc di Gregorio? And also that some dude got shot outside your flat, but let's start with Marc. I tried to text you, but the message failed, so I screamed in excitement or frustration or whatever, and a hunky cowboy came over to see what the problem was. Let's just say that not everything about Wyoming is awful."

"You hooked up with a cowboy?"

"We're talking about *your* sex life today, not mine."

"I didn't hook up with Marc di Gregorio."

"Awwwww, boo. I figured there was a fifty-fifty chance. I mean, you look so hot together."

"He did ask, but I turned him down."

"You...what? For a second there, I thought you said you turned down Marc di Gregorio."

"I did."

"Have you lost your mind? Are you sick? Running a fever?"

"He's not my type."

"Honey, have you seen that chiselled jaw? He's everybody's type. I have straight male friends who would turn for him."

"I'll admit he's very handsome, but he's not Owen."

"Owen? Wait, wait... Gummy Bear Guy? Did you fix things after your dumb-ass courier comment?"

"It's a long story..." I started at the beginning with the tentative steps Owen and I had taken back into each other's lives, all the way through to the dead body and Owen's late-night rescue mission. "So, here I am, waiting for him to get back from Peterborough."

Tuesday evening, and it was the first chance I'd had to take a good look around. The garden had to be an acre in size, and there was a triple garage at the back. A cleaner came on Fridays, he said, and the gardener worked Mondays. Moose was staying with a neighbour while Owen was away, but I thought I might have seen him this morning as I walked to the train station, a medium-sized black lab who'd seemed puzzled as I slipped out of Owen's gate. The lady with Moose had looked me up and down as well, but all she'd said was, "Good morning."

"You're in his house? Alone?"

"He gave me a key."

"Whoa."

"Exactly."

"Is it nice? The house?"

"It's literally my dream home." Big, but not so big that you'd get lost or knackered traipsing from one end to the other. Tidy, clean, and tastefully decorated. Not too many nooks and crannies for spiders to hide in, which had always been a hazard when I lived with my family in the old farm cottage. "There's a bathroom with a whirlpool tub big enough to swim in. I'm so, so tempted to have a soak."

And I deserved a pick-me-up after Priscilla's bitching tonight. She hadn't been happy that Alice had "won" Richard two nights in a row, and she'd still been whining to Patrick about how unfair it all was when I left the theatre with Marc. He'd asked his driver to drop me off at the train station so I didn't have to walk. Despite a rocky start, I thought I might actually come out of this six-week nightmare with two more friends, one old and one new.

"Go and have a soak, then. Owen will never know."

"Even if he did, he wouldn't mind. He said to make myself at home."

"So what's stopping you?"

Nothing. Nothing was stopping me. Both my cottage and the flat only had showers, and a long, hot bath would be heavenly. I carried on talking to Viola as I headed up the stairs—the giant bathtub would probably take an hour to fill.

"Okay, okay, I'll take a bath. Is this your subtle way of saying I stink?"

"No, but I expect pictures so I can live vicariously through you."

"Honey, I'm just not that kind of girl."

"Of the bathroom, idiot. And the rest of the house. You know I'm a nosy cow."

The bathroom door swung open on silent hinges, and I let out a long breath. This was the nicest place I'd ever stayed, unless you counted the handful of nights I'd spent in a five-star hotel in New York. But that was a pity upgrade. The production company had booked us into a three-star place, but after a little fire and a lot of water damage, other establishments in the area had taken in the poor lost souls who found themselves on the sidewalk in the middle of the night. Still, the complimentary toiletries and the candy on my pillow had been lovely, even if I couldn't get the smell of smoke out of my clothes.

"Okay, fine, I'll show you the bathroom."

Owen wouldn't mind, would he? I mean, he live-streamed his squirrel.

Viola squealed when I switched to FaceTime. "OMG! It's massive."

"I told you it was. And don't ask me what all the buttons in the shower do because I have no idea."

"You could fit a whole rugby team in there."

"I definitely won't be doing that."

"Think about it... All those soapy muscles and—"

"Viola!" I pushed down the plug and flipped on the taps. "I knocked back Marc di Gregorio because I'm still hung up on Owen; I'm not going to invite a local sports team over for sexy time. Hmm, what I really need is bubble bath."

"Check the cupboards. He might have some."

"I doubt that. Bubble bath's a bit girly, isn't it, and Owen's definitely all m—" I threw open the cupboard next to the bath. "Oh, he does."

Three different kinds, in fact. Rose and ylang-ylang, orange and bergamot, geranium and gingerlily, and the bottles looked like the fancy, expensive kind.

"Maybe he's one of those metrosexuals," Viola said.

"I suppose he must be."

What other explanation could there be?

I found out a minute later.

The tub was full of bubbles, the bathroom was full of steam, and I needed a towel. Or two towels, just in case my hair got wet. I found the airing cupboard on the third try and pulled out a fluffy pale-pink bath sheet. I could do laundry tomorrow morning. Patrick had taken pity on us and agreed to a later start, probably because the make-up artist kept complaining about eye bags.

"Oh, that's Owen's," I muttered without thinking. The embroidered "HIS" in the corner was the giveaway.

"Huh?" Viola said. "Who does the 'HERS' belong to?"

"What?"

"Those things come in pairs. His and Hers. People give them as wedding presents."

"No, Owen isn't married." He hadn't been wearing a ring; I would have noticed. But when I pulled out the next towel and found "HERS," my heart stuttered.

"What the...?"

His 'n' hers towels, bubble bath... My mind raced. Owen was married? Divorced? Then why was her stuff still here? Oh my goodness.

"Babes, I'm so sorry."

"I can't believe this."

"Why do all the good ones turn out to be scum?"

"Owen isn't scum. He never said he wasn't involved with anyone. I just assumed..."

Assumed wrongly. And when I thought about it logically, it would have been more surprising if Owen didn't have a girlfriend. He was handsome, well-off, and kind.

"Well, it's still the sort of thing he should have mentioned. Haven't you been talking to him for weeks now?"

"Yes, but...but we've been sticking to safe topics."

I'd been sticking to safe topics. Work, hobbies, the weather. Nothing that might lead to me blurting out my feelings and scaring him off for good. And when he'd invited me to stay here, he'd treated me as a friend. Offered me the guest room, made me a drink, given me a key. Okay, the fact that the alarm code was my birthday was a little odd, but maybe he'd just needed a memorable date that nobody else would guess? And my birthday parties *had* been memorable. Like the time we'd tried to bake a cake and ended up dropping a carton of eggs. I'd slipped over in the mess and ended up in A&E with a bruised coccyx.

"What are you going to do?" Viola asked.

"I'll have to talk to him."

Last time, I'd gone for avoidance, but I wouldn't be making *that* mistake again.

"Good luck."

"Thanks; I'm going to need it."

I was terrible at the deep and meaningful stuff. My longest relationship had lasted seven months, and for the last two of those, I'd been desperately trying to work out how to let him down gently. Then he'd accidentally texted me a dick pic instead of sending it to his other girlfriend, and I'd called him every sucky name I could think of and several I invented. He told me to grow up, and I threw a library book at him. A hardback, thankfully. At least I got something right.

But when I tried to call Owen again that Tuesday night —twice—there was no answer.

The make-up artist was going to hate me in the morning.

Twelve

The sound of a slamming door woke me.

My first thought was "axe murderer," and my second thought was "cleaner." But it was only Wednesday, wasn't it? Unless I'd slept for three days. In which case, the axe murderer would probably be easier to placate than Patrick Sheridan.

My third thought was "Owen."

Maybe he'd decided to surprise me again?

He hadn't.

I ran downstairs in my Barbie pyjamas—which I hadn't bought, honest, they were a joke present from Viola—tripped down the last two steps, and landed on my arse in front of a perfectly coiffed blonde. Her disdainful expression reminded me of Priscilla, and she didn't offer a hand to help me up.

"Uh, who are you?"

The alarm wasn't wailing, so she obviously knew my birthday. Or perhaps she was an evil tech genius? Did axe murderers come in female?

"I was about to ask you the same question."

"I'm Serena. A friend of Owen's. There was a small problem with my accommodation, and he said I could stay here for a few days." And now I was babbling. "Who are you?"

"Rosamund. Owen's fiancée."

Fiancée. All night, I'd been trying to convince myself that my fears were unfounded. That Owen just liked bubble bath and he'd bought the towels in a charity shop. Or that he hadn't noticed the whole "his 'n' hers" thing and he'd simply liked the colour. But now here she was. Rosamund. The diamond on her finger didn't lie.

"Right, uh, congratulations."

"Thank you. Serena? Now I recall... An old schoolfriend?" She peered down at me. "The walking disaster?"

She gave a posh little *hu-hu-hu* laugh, but it wasn't funny. The walking disaster? That was how Owen had described me? Yes, it was accurate, but it still stung. It stung even more when I was kneeling at the feet of his soon-to-be wife.

"Yes, that's me," I said brightly, calling on every bit of my acting experience to not look as if I were dying inside. "I've always been a bit clumsy."

"Well, don't let me stop you from whatever it is you were trying to do."

"I thought I'd just make some coffee before I go to work."

"I'll take mine with one sweetener and a splash of skimmed milk. Let me know if you struggle with the coffee machine—I realise it can be a little complicated."

It was a freaking Nespresso machine. All I had to do was pop in a pod and push the button. This woman might have been Owen's dearly beloved, and yes, I'd only met her two minutes ago, but I already hated her.

"I'll try to remember that."

She swished past me in her crease-free cream shift dress and matching cape, and I scrambled to my feet. Why hadn't Owen warned me? Why hadn't he mentioned the dragon lady would be coming home? I could have been prepared with a witty comeback to her underhand insults.

In the kitchen, I shoved a decaf pod into the machine, fumed as it hissed away, and then dumped three teaspoons of sugar and a generous serving of whole milk into a mug. Rosamund was sitting in the living room, reading a lifestyle magazine, and I was careful to slosh coffee over the edges of the mug when I slammed it down beside her.

"Whoops, how inept of me."

"Thank you. How long are you planning on staying? I'm having friends over for a soirée on Friday evening."

The unspoken words? *And you're not invited.*

Which was fine. I didn't want to be here, not with the Priscilla clone and a "friend" who didn't even have the decency to mention his significant other. Would it really have been so hard to tell me about his upcoming freaking wedding?

"Only for another hour or so. I'm going to stay in London tonight."

"Be careful when you leave—the steps outside can be slippery when they're wet."

This had been a mistake. Thinking that I could erase eight years of stupidity and pick up where I left off with Owen was a monumental error. And I was talking Giza Pyramid sized. Of course he'd changed—it was me who'd stayed stuck in the past, but no more. New Serena was going to be upbeat, and adventurous, and look where she was putting her feet.

New Serena was going to rock.

"What's with the suitcase?" Marc asked, and all the tears I'd been holding back escaped in one go. Dammit! So much for staying upbeat. "Things didn't work out with the guy?"

"N-n-no. No, they didn't." He steered me into a quiet corner and wiped my cheeks with the bottom of his T-shirt. Which didn't help much, but it was the thought that counted. "His fiancée showed up this morning."

"His fiancée?" Marc's eyebrows winged up to his hairline. No Botox for him. "You were chasing an engaged man?"

"Obviously I didn't know he was engaged. He conveniently left that part out."

"That's low."

"The absolute lowest."

"What did he say? Don't tell me he tried to justify it."

"He didn't say anything. He's away on business."

Owen had sent one text while I was on the train—*Sorry, the lack of sleep caught up with me last night. Hope the play went well*—and I'd ignored it, of course.

"The fiancée just showed up? They don't live together?"

"It seems not, but she must spend plenty of time there. I accidentally used half a bottle of her bubble bath last night. Rose and ylang-ylang."

"What is ylang-ylang anyway? One of my many, many exes wanted to call our future kid that."

"I think it's a kind of tree." I managed a tiny smile. "Ylang-ylang? That poor girl would have been bullied terribly at school."

"That's exactly what I said. Don't mention baby names in front of Patrick—his wife's pregnant, and her favourites so far are Wisteria for a girl and Branch for a boy."

"Branch?"

"Shh. It's a sore point." Marc gave my hand a squeeze. "Do you need a place to stay tonight?"

"I was going to try booking.com."

He gave a sly grin. "I have a spare bedroom in my suite if you want to send a big 'fuck you' to the jackass. Or if you prefer, I can ask my assistant to make separate arrangements."

A part of me wanted to wallow in misery alone—okay, not totally alone, with Ben & Jerry for company—but I did like the "fuck you" idea. Not just for Owen but for Rosamund too. She thought I was a useless fool, but thanks to Marc, I could be a useless fool with a hot heartthrob on my arm. The reporters were still hanging around in droves. All I had to do was not fall on my arse again.

"If I stay in your spare bedroom, do you promise not to try any funny business?"

"Define 'funny business.'" He crossed his eyes and puffed out his cheeks. "How about this? Is this okay?"

I poked him in the chest. "Clothing is to be worn at all times."

"Even in the shower? Could be awkward."

"As long as I'm not in the bathroom, you're allowed to strip off to bathe, but I'm definitely not getting naked with you."

Marc clasped both hands over his chest. "You break my heart, but it's a deal."

At least I'd come out of this mess with one friend. Marc was sweeter than I'd ever imagined he would be, and there was no better man to hammer home the message that I'd moved on.

My phone buzzed in my pocket, and I froze. Then I checked the screen. Owen was calling. Seriously? He'd abandoned me to his fiancée's meanness, and now he wanted to chat?

No. Just no.

"Is that him?" Marc asked.

I nodded. "I'm not going to answer it."

But Marc did. Before I could stop him, he grabbed the phone out of my hand and put it to his ear.

"Serena's answering service. ... Nah, man, she's in the bathroom. ... Hey, angel, are you done in there? Women, they take forever doing their hair. ... Sure, I'll tell her you called." He tucked the phone back into my pocket. "Owen called."

"Yes, I got that. What did he say?"

"Not much, just asked to speak with you. He sounded worried."

I bet he did. His secret was out now. But why had he kept his engagement quiet in the first place? Why hadn't he told me about Rosamund and introduced the two of us? Yes, I'd have been disappointed that he could never be mine, but now I was disappointed in him as a person. He'd acted so underhand about the whole thing. Even a friendship would feel weird when he'd hidden something so important.

A text popped up a moment later.

OWEN

Where are you? We need to talk.

The hell we did.

ME

I realise we've been out of each other's lives for a while, but you could at least have warned me about Rosamund. I'd have found somewhere else to stay sooner.

OWEN

I can explain. Please, just call me.

He could explain? Really? Well, I could block him. I needed to focus on work. There were still three weeks left on stage, and if Detective Cartwright didn't return to Willowbrook, I'd have to find a new job as well. Owen could focus on computers and wedding planning—surely that was plenty to keep him busy?

I had my own life now, and he wasn't welcome in it.

Thirteen

Screw the world.
    Screw everyone.

A day and a half later, and Marc's laissez-faire attitude was starting to rub off on me. There was no point in fretting over what I couldn't control. On Wednesday, we'd headed for his hotel suite amid an explosion of camera flashes, polished off a good bottle of wine between us, and fallen asleep on the couch.

Yesterday morning, we'd walked along the South Bank and ridden on the London Eye, and then I'd thrown myself into the role of the other woman in the evening. Alice was winning four-nil, and Priscilla was pissed. So pissed that she'd called me a selfish witch in the hallway afterwards, furious that I was "hogging the limelight," and accused me of using my relationship with Marc to "raise my profile."

We'd nearly come to blows when I'd told her a few home truths. That even with all her acting experience, Eliza didn't come across as likeable, and if she was a bit nicer, she might get more votes. Carla had stepped in to act as referee while Marc steered me out to the waiting limo.

Did I regret my words?

I regretted not waiting until the final performance because I still had to put up with Priscilla for three more weeks, but someone needed to put that diva in her place, and nobody else seemed willing. Not even Patrick. Feather had just stood there gawking, and Andi gave me a thumbs up but kept her mouth shut.

This morning, Marc had treated me to breakfast at a bistro near the hotel, and his companionship was the only reason I didn't completely regret signing up for *The Other Woman*. Last night, over another bottle of wine, we'd had a heart-to-heart, and he'd confessed that he found our platonic relationship hard. That it was the first time in years he'd been alone with a woman and remained fully clothed. Then he'd started on the whisky and let slip that he'd been in love once—just once—but she'd enlisted in the army and broken up with him when she got deployed.

The world thought he was a womaniser, but really, he was only guarding his heart.

And he was helping to protect mine too.

Tonight should have heralded my joyful reunion with Owen, but instead, I was hiding backstage, praying that he wouldn't actually be dumb enough to use the ticket he'd bought. I figured it was unlikely—presumably, he'd be expected at Rosamund's soirée—but he'd already proven that he wasn't quite as smart as I'd always assumed.

"Chin up, Carlisle," Marc said. "I'd say 'break a leg,' but I'm worried you might take it literally."

A moment later, Priscilla walked past and showed a smile that looked suspiciously genuine. Had she been practising in front of the mirror all day?

"Break a leg, Serena."

"You too."

"That was weird," Marc muttered after she was out of earshot.

"She's faking. There's no way she turned human overnight."

"You don't think your little speech yesterday hit a nerve?"

"Not in a million years. What was the movie where the aliens studied humans and then adapted themselves to fit in better? She'd have been great in that."

"Give it a few years, and there'll be a remake. You ready?"

"No."

"Get out there and win me again. I'd rather tongue-fuck you than Miss Extra-Terrestrial."

"Has anyone ever told you how charming you are?"

"Thousands and thousands of people, all of whom want something from me." Marc kissed me on the cheek. "Good luck."

It was a wasted sentiment. When I walked out on stage and scanned the dimly lit audience, the first thing I saw was Owen Cadwallader watching me from the front row, and he looked far from happy. No, he was half-peeved, half-concerned, half-I-want-to-jump-on-stage-and-spank-you. Wait, was that three halves? Maths never had been my strong point. Anyhow, there was unmistakable heat in his gaze, and that threw me off balance.

He had no right to look at me that way, not when he was engaged to another woman.

But look at me, he did. His gaze was so intense that I stumbled over both my words and my own feet. Marc caught me and made it look as if the trip was supposed to happen, but I couldn't focus on my performance at all. It was no surprise when Priscilla won the public vote for the first time. In fact, it was quite a relief. The less time I had to spend on the receiving end of Owen's stare, the better. Sweat was trickling down my back, and even when I wasn't looking in his direction, I could feel him there, a presence I couldn't escape.

"That was an experience," Marc muttered when we came off stage after the third act. "Whatever's going on with the fiancée, I'd say the jackass still has feelings for you."

"He can have all the feelings he wants. They're not reciprocated."

Of course, Carla was listening in. "Did you know there's a fine line between love and hate?"

"Please, spare me the psychobabble."

"Just trying to help."

"Just don't." I tore off Alice's sweater and managed to inhale a piece of mohair when the thing got stuck over my head. Mental note: undo the buttons first. I began coughing, and Marc had to rescue me.

"Breathe, sweetheart. I've got you."

When my head finally popped out, Priscilla was rolling her eyes. "Can you be quiet? Some of us are trying to concentrate."

See? Told you she was faking the pleasantries.

"I'm not"—*cough*—"doing this for fun."

She thrust her glass of water at me. "Drink this. I haven't touched it."

I swallowed the entire glassful and sagged against the wall. As soon as Marc finished with the finale, we could escape back to the hotel. We were definitely going to need more wine tonight. I had no idea how much the Château Lafite Rothschild we'd been drinking cost, but Marc had told me not to worry about it.

Although perhaps I wouldn't need to polish off an entire bottle. Now that I'd put some distance between myself and Owen, the tension was ebbing away, and I felt weirdly relaxed. Slightly sick too, but mainly sleepy. I sank into a chair and let my head flop back against the wall. At least Priscilla was taking more of the load today, which made both of us happy. Maybe not Marc, because he'd told me in confidence that Priscilla kissed like an eel, and I'd asked him how many eels he'd kissed, and he said only one when he was drunk and his high-school buddies had dared him. I hadn't kissed any eels, so in that respect, I was woefully inexperienced. And I also wasn't going to kiss Priscilla, thank goodness. Whoa, I really did feel tired... Would Marc do the whole Prince Charming thing and carry me out to the car? There'd be cameras, and Owen, and Owen would do that angry-face thing, which was actually kind of hot, although I'd never admit that because he wasn't my friend anymore.

"Are you okay?"

Andi looked a little blurry, and I tried to nod. How long had I been sitting here? It felt like forever and no time at all.

"Tired. So tired. Long day."

"You need to take off your costume."

"Give me... Give me a minute."

I'd already taken some of it off, but the rest... Where had all my strength gone? Had my blood sugar dropped? What I needed was a gummy bear. Owen always used to carry a packet that he claimed were "for emergencies," but really they were more of a snack.

A woman crouched beside me, a woman with blonde hair. Carla?

"Are you okay?"

Why did people keep asking me that? "Fine. Tired."

"Fuck, Serena. What's wrong?"

Marc sounded worried. Why was he worried? Was he acting? He was an excellent actor. And a good kisser too, except now my lips felt weird. As if they didn't fit together properly. All of me felt weird. I slumped sideways, and maybe I'd have landed on the floor—*break a leg, Serena*—but Marc caught me. There was Prince Charming. He should definitely do one of those cartoon movies.

"Someone call a doctor."

Who needed a doctor? What was wrong? I didn't need a doctor. I merely needed to sleep for five or six months.

"Brother is...doctor," I mumbled, just in case that helped.

"Has she been drinking?" a disembodied voice asked.

No, no, nooooo, not at work. I was a professional.

"Not that I saw," Priscilla said. "But alcoholics can be good at hiding their transgressions."

"Don't be such a bitch," Marc told her. "Serena isn't an alcoholic."

"Is she diabetic?" another voice questioned. "Any history of fainting? Heart problems? Low blood pressure?"

I tried to tell them no, I was as healthy as a horse, but no words came out. Everything was fuzzy.

"I have no idea," Marc said. "But I know somebody who might be able to help."

Who? My brother? But he was in the Caribbean. And my parents never answered the phone late at night, which left... *No.* I tried to explain that I'd rather take my chances with a paramedic, but before I could croak out a protest, the fog rolled in and everything went blank.

Fourteen

A h, this was better. I was in a bed now. Not a very comfortable one, and someone had left the lights on —and what was that bloody awful beeping?—but at least I wasn't propped up in a chair anymore. Why did my throat hurt so much? Water... I needed water. With some effort, I forced my eyes open, and...oh, I was having a nightmare.

Brilliant.

I quickly closed them again.

"You can't hide that easily," Owen said.

"What are you doing here?"

Wherever "here" was.

"You passed out, and nobody else knew your medical history. If you think I'm leaving you to lie in hospital alone, then you're sorely mistaken."

"Shouldn't...shouldn't you be at a soirée?"

"Why would I be at a soirée?"

"Because your fiancée—"

"I don't know where my *ex*-fiancée is, and until Wednesday, when she showed up at my home in an attempt to ruin my life, I didn't care."

"Your ex-fiancée?" My brain was still full of sludge. "But she said—"

"She lied. The big downside of living in a small village is that everyone talks. I didn't realise she was still friendly with my dog-sitter, and the dog-sitter told her that I was away and you were staying in my house. I also didn't realise that she still had a key. The locks have been changed now, but...fuck. I should have told you about her, I know I should, but I didn't want to own up to what a fool I'd been."

"She had a ring. A diamond."

"Well, I don't know where she got it, because she threw the one I gave her back at me."

Oh. "You're honestly not together?"

"We broke up before Christmas. And then you came back into my life, and I thought it was fate. Don't walk away, Serena. Please, don't walk away." He reached for my hand, and when he squeezed it at a funny angle, I realised there was an IV running into it. What had happened to me? "I already lost you once, and if it happens again..." He trailed off and shook his head.

"But her bubble bath is in your home. Her towels."

Blank look. "Her what?"

"Unless you're a fan of ylang-ylang?"

"I don't even know what that is. But I don't take baths, and my cleaner looks after the laundry."

Could he really be that clueless? I thought back to the time my dad accidentally bought a butt plug for my mum because both he and Margaret who ran the charity shop thought it was an ornament. Yes, it was possible.

"Can you start at the beginning? No lies this time."

"I only ever lied by omission. Which I realise isn't much better than lying outright, but... Yes, I'll start from the beginning." Owen took a couple of steadying breaths. "After we lost touch, I didn't date much. I went to uni as you know, graduated with first-class honours, and then landed a job with a small tech start-up. My parents wanted me to carry on in academia and get a PhD, but I'd had enough of studying. The start-up... I enjoyed the work but not the management style. The board had 'shiny new object' syndrome, and nothing ever got finished. So I moved to HC Systems. It's not as glamorous as showbiz, but I fit in there."

"Showbiz isn't glamourous. My best friend is a make-up artist, and she just spent two weeks communing with raccoons in Wyoming."

"Raccoons are probably more fun than staring at code until your eyes hurt. But I like the challenge of keeping hackers out, and I worked my way up the ladder into a managerial position. Which meant networking, and I met Rosamund at a local business breakfast. She owns an interior design consultancy."

Yes, I could picture that. She seemed like exactly the kind of woman to judge by appearance.

"I didn't see her as your type."

Owen grimaced. "She's a good actress. Not as good as you, but still... She's very charming when she wants something."

"And she wanted you?"

"Unfortunately. Being in a relationship was okay at first. I was working long hours, although she gradually shuffled my schedule around to accommodate the things she wanted to do. My parents loved her, which I suppose should have been a huge red flag, and Mum told me she'd make the perfect wife for a CEO, which is what they both wanted me to become. But I'm happy where I am. Anyhow, I just coasted along for far longer than I should have."

"You asked her to marry you. That's hardly coasting."

Did I sound bitter? That's probably because I was.

"No, she asked me. At a summer garden party, in front

of a hundred guests including our families. I said yes because I didn't want to embarrass both of us, and then I struggled to find a way out. Things got worse after the engagement party. I guess she thought that with a diamond on her finger, she didn't need to try so hard to hide who she really was. The situation finally came to a head this past December." Owen gave a heavy sigh. "Luke held a Christmas party at his place, family and friends, fifty people or so. Rosamund had a run-in with his ex."

"Is this the axe-throwing ex?"

"The one and only, but thankfully, she didn't have an axe on that occasion. Usually, Rosamund stays composed in public, but that day, the gloves came off, and I decided enough was enough. To cut a long story short, she spent Christmas with my parents while I ate pizza with Moose, and ever since then, Ros and my mother have been working together to convince me I made a mistake." His lopsided smile made the heart-rate monitor beat funny. "You've always been a sore point."

"Why? I know your mum thought I was a dumb klutz, but I wasn't even there."

"Not in person, maybe, but you were still in my life. I refused to change the alarm code, for starters. That annoyed Ros. I never missed an episode of *Whispers in Willowbrook*. And then there's this..."

Before I could process, he whipped off his shirt, and holy cannoli, the man had abs. Abs and pecs. And was that... was that... I tried to sit up, but a wave of nausea made me rethink that idea, so I beckoned him closer instead.

"You tattooed a gummy bear on your chest?"

"On my heart. It was always you, Serena. Ros had to look at it every time we..." His cheeks turned red. "...you know. She kept telling me I should get it removed. Said it was childish."

The tears were back. I tried to wipe them away with a hand, but the stupid IV tube got caught. Owen stepped in with a handkerchief.

"Why didn't you say something?"

"What was I supposed to say? 'Hey, beautiful, I know it's been eight years, but I'm still crazily in love with you and no other woman will ever measure up'? I didn't want you to run a mile, and besides, you're already spoken for."

"I am?"

"Marc di Gregorio?"

"Oh, no, no, no. I'm not dating Marc. I've never even kissed him outside of work."

"You looked remarkably cosy having breakfast this morning. The pictures were all over the internet."

Now it was my turn to blush. "I just wanted to make you jealous."

"Mission accomplished."

My brain was struggling to keep up. Owen wasn't engaged, and Rosamund wasn't the love of his life. Perhaps I was? He had a freaking gummy bear inked over his heart, and it was a red one. My favourite. It matched the one he'd gifted me all those years ago. All those years ago when he used to eat the yellow ones because they were the flavour I liked least and leave the raspberry ones for me. Almost unconsciously, my fingers went to my neck, but the familiar comfort of the waxed cord was missing. My heart stuttered, and the machine beeped faster in sympathy.

"It's in my pocket," Owen assured me. "One of the nurses took it off."

Thank goodness. "You...you love me?"

"That will never change."

"Ditto. When you offered to go to the prom with me, that was the best moment of my life, and then it all went so wrong, and I just... I just..."

"It's okay."

"Is it? I still haven't paid you back for the cost of the solicitor."

"He was a family friend, and besides, I think I can cover it. HC offers great stock options. And if it's any consolation, I nearly got arrested last night when I insisted on staying with you. Technically, it's past visiting hours and only next of kin are allowed."

"How did you convince them to make an exception?"

"I didn't. After I explained the Rosamund situation, Marc di Gregorio charmed the nurse manager. Apparently, she's a fan."

"Marc came too?"

"Briefly. He'll be back in the morning. He helped out on the condition that I apologise, so here I am, telling you I'm so fucking sorry for everything that happened. I wish we could turn back the clock."

"Me too. I'm still not entirely sure what did happen last night. One minute, I was fine, and the next...lights out."

"Someone roofied you."

Had I heard him right? They *what*? "Roofied me?"

"Rohypnol. The medical team pumped your stomach and gave you a drug that reverses the effects of benzodiazepines."

"But who...? How?"

"It was in the water you drank. Priscilla actually did get arrested, but she'll probably be out on bail by the morning."

That...that was almost unbelievable, but when I screwed my eyes shut, a fleeting memory came back. *Priscilla complaining about my coughing. Priscilla handing me her glass of water.* Why would she roofie me? True, we couldn't stand each other, but didn't she realise that if she got caught —*when* she got caught—it would only harm her career in the end?

"I think... I think it was *her* drink. It wasn't meant for me."

"So she claims, but one of the production people—Feather?—said she saw Priscilla drop something into the glass after she poured it."

Another memory... *Priscilla suggesting I might be an alcoholic.* Had she simply been trying to make me look bad in front of everyone? Was she aiming for woozy and got the dosage wrong? She wasn't a bad actress, just a horrible person.

"What will happen now?"

"With the play? I'm no expert, but don't you both have understudies?"

"Stand-ins, yes."

"So Priscilla's stand-in will take over, I imagine, and you'll go back on stage when you feel well enough."

"And what about..." I closed my eyes for a moment and braced for disappointment. "What about us?"

Was there even an "us"?

Owen didn't answer, not in words. No, he leaned closer, closer, and brushed his lips across mine. Heat zinged through my veins, and for crying out loud, would someone shut that bloody beeping off?

"Come home with me. You can meet Moose, and then we can burn all the towels."

"I love you," I whispered. "Even more than gummy bears."

"I love you too."

He kissed me again, and this time, he rivalled Marc's on-stage persona. No, he surpassed it. A little tongue, a lot of fire, and if a nurse hadn't cleared her throat from the doorway, my paper gown would have ended up in shreds.

"Sir, we're already bending the rules for you to be here. I'm going to have to ask you to put your shirt back on."

"I do apologise."

A giggle threatened to burst free. I tried to swallow it and ended up having a coughing fit, but thankfully this time, Priscilla wasn't on hand with water. Owen passed me a plastic cup with a straw, and I sipped until I could breathe steadily again.

Tonight, I'd go home with Owen. Although I was already at home. *He* was my home. My safe place, my rock, my best friend, and now—with luck—my partner for life.

I'd just have to remember to unblock his number on my phone.

Fifteen

> There was drama off stage at Friday's performance of The Other Woman as one cast member allegedly drugged another. Priscilla Prentice, rumoured to be embroiled in a bitter feud over the affections of Marc di Gregorio with her co-star, Serena Carlisle, is said to have slipped a date-rape drug into Ms. Carlisle's drink right before the final act.
>
> The show concluded an hour later than planned with a stand-in, but some disgruntled audience members have requested a refund. "I didn't pay fifty quid to sit around listening to sirens for an hour," said one man who wished to remain anonymous.
>
> We understand that Serena Carlisle will be rejoining the cast on Monday, but Priscilla Prentice has been sidelined for good.

S eemed celebgossip.com was on the case. I'd been given the weekend off to recover, not so much from the drugs but from the soreness in my throat. The audience deserved to have actors who could perform without coughing their guts up. The doctors had discharged me early this morning, which gave me two and a half days of R&R before Monday's performance. I was under strict instructions not to talk too much, and what better way to heed medical advice than to snuggle up with Owen and watch Netflix?

We had ice cream, chocolate, and gummy bears, plus doggy treats for Moose. Owen had fired his dog-sitter, so Moose would be splitting his time between home and Owen's office for the next few weeks. Luckily, nobody at HC Systems minded well-behaved pets, and Owen said one of the programmers even brought a pair of sugar gliders to work in her pocket. But at the moment, Moose was stretched out on the sofa with his head resting on my thigh, snoring softly.

"I always thought Netflix and chill meant, you know, watching Netflix and chilling out," he said.

"No way."

"Yes way. When colleagues asked me whether I had plans at the weekend, I always wondered why they looked at me funny when I answered. I'm surprised no one reported me to HR."

"How did you find out what it actually meant?"

"Luke's sister." Owen covered his eyes with his hands. "She asked what I was doing at the weekend, I said Netflix and chilling with Ros, and Tia said she didn't think Ros was the type. So I said that actually, she was a big fan of *Bridgerton*. Then I was informed of the error of my ways."

And I was hooting with laughter. Which did nothing

for my cough or my headache, but did feel pretty damn good after everything that had happened.

"Just so you know, I *am* the type for Netflix and chilling, but I prefer romcoms."

Owen moved his hands. "Oh, really?"

"I'm not trying to rush you or anything, but...yes."

"How are you feeling?"

"At this moment? I'm feeling like I've been waiting eight years to see you naked. If I have to wait a few extra days, then I will, but I don't want to."

Owen leapt to his feet in one smooth move, and a second later, I was in his arms. My favourite place in the world. The journey home had been bumpy, but now that I'd arrived, the potholes faded into the background.

"Let's focus on the 'and chill' part for today. Moose, stay here."

I tossed him a biscuit. "Good boy."

Owen carried me all the way to his bedroom, to the king-sized bed with pale grey sheets and a padded velvet headboard. I'd always avoided looking directly at his package in the past—unless his attention was elsewhere, anyway— but now I was free to stare openly. Sheesh, he was hard already. And roughly the size of London's Gherkin if the outline in his grey sweatpants was anything to go by.

"When you said 'chill,' how cold were you talking?" I asked. "Pimm's at a garden party? Slow, sedate glacier? Or full-on beastly liquid nitrogen?"

"Liquid helium."

"Uh, so I'm not sure if that's good or bad."

"It's colder than liquid nitrogen."

Of course he would know that. "Thanks for clearing that up."

We stared at each other for a beat and then began tearing at each other's clothes, years of pent-up frustration coming to a head in the ripping of fabric. My fingernails and determination versus Owen's raw strength meant we ended up naked at the same time, and he threw me onto the bed. *Threw* me. I'd never been so turned on in my life. Or so wet. My thighs were slick, and he'd barely even touched me yet.

Holy Toledo, he had hip grooves, a deep V pointing the way to his perfect specimen of a cock. I lay breathless, drinking him in, but not for long. He only gave me a second before he parted my legs and showed me that his cock wasn't the only magic part of his anatomy. The sight of his head buried between my thighs nearly made me come on the spot. I arched off the bed as heat surged through me, gripping the sheets with both hands at my sides.

"I've been waiting forever to taste you," he murmured, his breath ticklish. "The wait was worth it."

"And I've been waiting forever for an Owen Cadwallader orgasm, so don't stop."

His chuckle sent another ripple of pleasure through me, and I gasped. I'd never been this sensitive before. Every touch, every stroke set off fireworks. The pleasure built and built, coiling inside my belly as my breath came in pants, my thoughts jumbled. When our gazes met, the intensity in Owen's undid me. *Mine.* He flicked his tongue one final time and the dam burst. I cried out as the orgasm blazed through me, and a moment later, we heard the scrabble of claws on tile.

"Shit!" Owen rolled off the bed and grabbed Moose before he could join in the fun. The dog thought it was a game and jinked sideways, and I laughed so hard I was practically crying as a naked Owen chased the excited mutt around the bedroom. Finally, he managed to wrestle Moose out the door, and this time he locked it.

"Fuck, I'm sorry," he said, panting slightly. "That's never happened before."

"It's a first for me too."

And then we were both laughing, but it was okay because we were Serena and Owen. Owen and Serena. We'd been friends forever, and above all, friends had fun. I grew serious again when Owen kissed me like he meant it, and the dog drama hadn't affected his dick. It was still as hard as granite.

"Don't you have somewhere you should be putting that thing?"

"You're not into foreplay?"

"I'm into everything, but if there's a choice right now, I'd rather you were into me."

"Then I'll find a condom."

I hesitated, but only for a second. "I'm on the pill."

"Are you saying...?"

"Just hurry up."

He sank into me bare, the first time I'd ever let a man do that, but it was the right man and the right time. The stretch made my breath hitch, and he gave me a moment to adjust to his size.

"Okay?" he asked.

"With you? Always."

He moved slowly at first, peppering my cheeks with delicate kisses. But as the pleasure built, that glorious tension, he thrust harder, his hands gripping my shoulders as I clawed at his peach of a backside. This time, the orgasm rolled over me like a wave and he followed me into the abyss, his gaze locked on mine.

Then we heard scratching at the door and dissolved into laughter again.

If the past five weeks had been a roller-coaster, the last fortnight had mostly been spent on the smooth sections. Fun, exhilaration, and a few bumps. Priscilla was gone, replaced by Tamara, who didn't have quite the same edge as Priscilla on stage but was a heck of a lot easier to get along with. The audience seemed to like her better, so I'd only had to perform the final scene with Marc eight times. In truth, it had been nice to share the load. Carla was still working out how to handle the change of actress in her study, but she'd been writing plenty of notes. I suspected that at some point, she'd pen a book about the drama behind the scenes and the psychological pressures of showbiz because that was where the real story lay. Meanwhile, the guy making the accompanying documentary had been walking around with a Cheshire cat grin for the past month.

A grin I mirrored. Because Owen had cleared out half of his closet and asked me to stay with him, at least until we knew what was going on with my career, and I'd said yes. Yes to living in Broxbourne, yes to waking up beside my best friend every morning. I hung up the phone, and Owen turned from the coffee machine, two mugs in his hands. The mugs had come from the gift shop at the theatre, and they had my freaking face on them.

"That didn't sound hopeful," he said.

"It was the police liaison officer. They're not going to charge Priscilla."

"How do you feel about that?"

We'd talked about it a lot. We'd talked about everything. There were no more secrets between us, only trust. I was in two minds over the Priscilla situation because while I wanted her to face justice, I'd also been dreading having to testify at a trial. Honestly, I just wanted the whole mess to go away.

"I'm okay with it. She's lost her job and been blacklisted

by every producer in the business, which for her is probably worse than a prison sentence anyway. Not that she'd have gone to prison. They'd only have given her a fine or community service."

There wasn't enough evidence, the liaison officer said. Yes, Priscilla had passed me the drink, and yes, Feather thought she'd seen her drop something into it, but she couldn't be certain it was even a pill. The documentary crew had caught me falling off the chair on tape, but not Priscilla pouring the glass of water or adding any foreign substances. No more drugs had been found in Priscilla's belongings, and she'd hired a good lawyer.

Owen nodded slowly. "I think it's the best outcome."

"And?"

"And what?"

"There's something else on your mind, I can tell."

This phase of our relationship might be new, but I'd known Owen for half my life, and in many ways, he hadn't changed a bit.

"This might be an unpopular opinion, but I think Priscilla's innocent."

"*What?* But last week, you offered to hire a law firm and bring a civil case."

"I did some more digging."

"Huh?"

"I might be in management now, but I started off in coding, and I still know my way around the interweb. Plus I have friends in low, low places. We wanted to make sure you weren't in any further danger, so we ran a few checks."

"What did you find?"

Owen took a seat opposite me and slid a mug across the kitchen table. The coffee was still too hot to drink, so I picked it up and blew on it, waiting.

"Feather's full name is Birdie Feather Lorratt." His quiet

snort told me what he thought of the name. "Her parents were both ornithologists. She decided to take a different path, and she used to go by Birdie. Six years ago, she was working as a stagehand on the Broadway adaptation of *The Hobbit* when she clashed with a young actress named Priscilla Prentice."

"What kind of clash did they have?"

"Someone found a baggie of cocaine backstage, and Birdie got the blame. She claimed it was Priscilla's, but nobody believed her."

"Yikes. I mean, I can understand why—Priscilla can be very convincing."

"The director's sister died from an overdose, and his stance on drugs bordered on militant, which meant the police got involved. But there wasn't enough evidence to charge Birdie. The upshot is that she got fired, and she found it difficult to get another job with that blot on her résumé."

The little pieces began to slot into place. "So she reinvented herself."

"I don't know whether it was a coincidence that she ended up working on *The Other Woman* with Priscilla or if that was her plan all along, but it put her in the perfect position for revenge."

"Priscilla was meant to drink the water."

"Exactly."

"Feather wanted to ruin her big moment."

"Yes, she did. And in the interests of full disclosure, it was meant to be *your* big moment. I, uh, tinkered with the app and switched a few of the votes."

A gasp escaped. "Why? Why would you do that?"

"Because I hated the idea of watching my woman kissing Marc di Gregorio."

"You..."

"Please don't throw the coffee at me. It's still quite hot."

Slowly, I put the cup down. I wasn't sure whether to hug Owen or yell at him, but in the end, I settled on civility. The knowledge that I'd always been his, even through the difficult times, made my heart sing.

"How many other times did you change the results?"

"None, I swear. But they haven't fixed the security flaw, so if you need an early night this week, just let me know."

"Carla would lose her mind if she found out."

"Then don't tell her."

I mimed zipping my lips together and throwing away the key. Then I unzipped them again because there was still so much we needed to discuss.

"What do you think I should do?"

"I think you should perform Act Four Monday through Friday, take a break and let Tamara do the honours on Saturday, and then go for glory in the final performance on Sunday."

"I meant about Feather, but you're okay with me snogging Marc now?"

"He's not quite the arsehole I assumed he would be."

The feeling was mutual. Last weekend, the three of us had eaten lunch together in the fancy five-star hotel to clear the air, and I'd been surprised at how well the two leading men in my life got along. They'd even talked about going to a rugby match together.

"He surprised me too. I actually feel a bit sorry for him —deep down, he wants to find happiness, but he's locked his heart up so tight that he can't."

"Someday, the right woman will come along with the key." Owen took a sip of his coffee, then cursed when he burned his lips. "And about Feather, I think you should do nothing. She's not a danger to you or anyone else."

"Do you think the cocaine was Priscilla's?"

"She went to rehab the year before last. Very quietly, but she was there for a month."

"And she just stood back while Feather got questioned by the police?"

"Feather spent three nights in jail. It was a rather large baggie."

"Wow. Well, in that case, I guess I can see where you're coming from. And who among us hasn't been tempted to roofie Priscilla at some point?"

"Precisely. Plus I bet if I dug deeper, I'd find out that Feather isn't the only intern who's suffered from Priscilla's underhandedness."

Wasn't that the truth? I'd overheard Carla talking to Patrick about Priscilla again the other day, and the words "batshit crazy" had been mentioned, along with "arrogant" and "self-centred." Her own hubris had been her downfall.

"Then we'll let sleeping dogs lie." I checked my watch. "Hurry up and drink your coffee. Put an ice cube in it or something. We still have an hour before I need to leave for the theatre, and you're wearing far too many clothes."

Sixteen

"You'll have to make up your mind. If we're going to the reunion, we needed to leave five minutes ago."

"A part of me wants to hold my head high and show everyone that I'm happy, but the other part would rather sit at home with Simone than face Libby Sieber."

We'd been on squirrel watch for days. Judging by the size of her, Simone was due to give birth at any moment. One of her fans had sent a tiny crib, which we'd duly installed on the bedroom windowsill, but she seemed to prefer her nest. And Simone was better company than ninety percent of my old schoolmates.

But dammit, I was a success, and I wanted to prove that. I'd received rave reviews for *The Other Woman*, the media had praised me for maintaining my dignity through the Priscilla scandal, and the day before yesterday, I'd nailed the finale with Marc. Okay, so rumours of a three-way were circulating after Owen and I passed out from fatigue and possible alcohol poisoning and spent Sunday night in Marc's hotel suite, but there were worse stories the paparazzi could have printed.

"Don't worry about Libby. She probably won't even be there."

"Oh?"

"Her latest boyfriend might have found out she was sending topless photos to another man. I'm sure he wasn't happy about it."

Over the past few weeks, I'd come to understand that while Owen was essentially still the sweet boy who'd pushed me on the garden swing until his arms hurt and packed jam sandwiches and crisps into his backpack so we could sneak off for a picnic, he'd also developed a greyness around the edges. While I was certain he didn't do anything entirely illegal, he did bend his morals occasionally.

"Did you have anything to do with the 'finding out' part?"

He flashed me a perfect grin. "I've been fucking with Libby for years. Call it a hobby."

"Really?"

His answer? He hummed a few bars from the Police's "Every Breath You Take."

"The divorce?"

"She needs to learn how to keep her clothes on."

Holy crap. Owen Cadwallader wasn't the boy I remembered. No, he was so, so much more.

"Uh, I don't suppose you fancy fucking with her ex-boyfriend as well? I found out why she was so upset that day —he had photos of me on his phone, the creep. I didn't even know he'd taken them."

"Darren Hendon?"

"Yes, him."

"Already done. He's serving nine years for distribution of child pornography."

"*What?*"

"He never did lose his taste for schoolgirls."

"Wait, did you...?"

"He should have used a better firewall." Owen held out a hand. "Let's go to the ball, my Valentine."

"But...but...I'm not even sure I have anything to wear."

"Follow me."

Just in case I'd been in any doubt over whether I had the perfect boyfriend, Owen proved me right yet again. Not only had he exacted the perfect revenge, but in a closet in the smallest of the spare bedrooms hung half a dozen beautiful dresses, all red, all in my size. Shoeboxes were stacked underneath, and there was even a selection of lingerie.

"What...? When...?"

"My PA had a busy weekend," Owen said, picking up a Black Lily bag. "But I chose these myself, for purely selfish reasons of course."

I peered inside and grinned when I saw the delicate scraps of lace. "You'll look great in thong panties."

"Only you will know my secret. Do you need help getting dressed?"

"No, because if you 'help,' we'll never go anywhere."

His eyes twinkled as he grinned, and I nearly changed my mind. But no, I'd go. It struck me that this would be the first event I'd ever been to where I didn't feel like a fraud. I'd proven I could act. I'd navigated the media minefield. I'd finally have the man of my dreams on my arm, and although there were still uncertainties to figure out—where I'd live long-term, for example, and where my next paycheck would come from—life was definitely heading in the right direction.

And not just my life.

Liam would be at tonight's reunion too, tanned, well-rested, and engaged. Yes, engaged. He'd asked Marissa to marry him on the beach in Antigua, and of course she'd said yes. I definitely wouldn't be buying him towels as a wedding present.

The his 'n' hers towels had been repurposed. Owen thought the offending items had most likely been an engagement gift, an overzealous guest jumping the gun at the lavish party Rosamund had insisted on throwing. Now the towels were in the mud room, and we used them to wipe Moose's paws after he came back from a walk. He had a new dog-sitter too, a lovely lady who'd given up work to care for her elderly mother and needed a little extra cash.

Speaking of Moose... He ran in, holding a box in his mouth, and dropped it at my feet. Owen groaned.

"What's that?" I stooped to look at the label. "Turkish delight?"

"*That* was supposed to be a surprise. Like gummy bears, but fancier."

"I mean, it is a surprise? Did you train him to fetch stuff?"

"No, he used his own initiative. Moose! Don't chew the ribbon."

"Aw, he's so cute. Are dogs allowed to eat Turkish delight?"

"Not the chocolate-covered ones."

I picked out a plain cube and offered it. Moose swallowed the treat in one go, then did a happy dance, his butt wiggling frantically. I totally understood how he felt, and it had nothing to do with the candy. Candy I'd eat later, after I'd squeezed into one of the beautiful dresses. My favourite had a ruched silhouette, a rounded neckline, and cap sleeves. The long skirt draped elegantly from a gold bar at the waist, and although it was a bit flashy for a school reunion, I was an actress. People would expect me to be OTT.

"This one?" I asked Owen.

"Perfect."

My parents were overjoyed at developments too, both at the prospect of Liam's wedding and that Owen had come back into my life. Into *our* lives. They'd always adored him. Although when I'd introduced Marc at the afterparty and he turned on the charm, I thought I'd detected a hint of wistfulness from Mum. But that hadn't lasted long. Half an hour later, she'd started dropping hints about two future weddings, and I'd been forced to step—gently—on her foot to get her to stop. Maybe someday Owen and I would tie the knot, but he'd just escaped from one engagement. No way was I scaring him off by pressuring him into another.

Contrary to common belief, I wasn't a fool.

No, I just took my time putting on a set of the beautiful lingerie he'd bought me, a flimsy black tulle thong with embroidered hearts and a matching bra that did wonders for my cleavage. I felt Owen's gaze on me the whole time I was getting ready, so I took my time slipping into the dress. A reverse striptease. Sexy and elegant and— Dammit, I couldn't do the zipper up.

"Can I borrow you for a second?"

Owen had put on a suit, charcoal grey and probably custom-tailored, and I almost reconsidered going out at all. He must have read my mind because he shook his head.

"Later."

"Spoilsport."

"Good things come to those who wait."

"Patience is my least favourite virtue."

"After last night, I thought that was chastity?"

Okay, he had me there. Last night, he'd had me everywhere. In the shower, over the kitchen counter, pressed up against the wall... I turned, and he pulled up the zipper. Then I felt something cold around my neck.

"What the...?"

It was a necklace. A beautiful ruby necklace. And the rubies were the shape of a gummy bear.

"Seven years ago, I designed a productivity app in my spare time. After ten months, I sold it to a bigger company, and I used the money to buy this. I've been waiting more than six years to put it around your neck, Serena."

This man, he was everything.

"You still thought we'd find our way back to each other?"

"Back then, yes. After four or five years, I began to lose hope, but it never quite disappeared completely."

"Don't make me cry. My mascara isn't waterproof."

The tears came anyway, but this time, they were brought by joy rather than sadness.

Seventeen

"Yikes!" Marissa whispered. "That's Libby Sieber?"

"Yup."

"She looks terrible."

I might have been biased, but yes, she absolutely did. Even worse than she had after the Carrie disaster, when I'd leapt on her and pulled out her stupid hair extensions, and then got arrested for the pleasure after one of my classmates freaked out at all the blood, called 999, and told them there was a murder in progress. Tonight, she had chewed nails and split ends, and she seemed generally worn around the edges. Oh, and she was obviously pregnant. That was a nice touch. When she looked up and saw me with Owen, Liam, and Marissa, she quickly averted her gaze and headed for the buffet table.

"I wonder who the father is?" I murmured. "From what I've heard, it might not be all that cut and dried."

Marissa's eyes widened. "Double yikes. That's going to make things tricky."

Inside, I gloated, but outside, I smiled politely as I made small talk with Owen at my side. I didn't need to lower myself to Libby-slash-Priscilla levels of bitchiness to get my revenge. Other people did that for me. Libby had once been Miss Popular, but now she was shunned. A dozen people told me how shocked they'd been about the Carrie incident. That it had made them see Libby for who she really was. Only a handful of attendees spoke to her, just her former hangers-on, and I heard them giggling about her downfall in the bathroom afterwards.

And it turned out that revelling in others' misfortune wasn't as satisfying as I'd always thought it would be. Libby looked utterly miserable, and I just felt kind of hollow inside. The happiness that warmed me when I looked at the ring on Marissa's finger and the smile on my brother's face was far more fulfilling.

I also realised that when it came to friends, quality trumped quantity every time. Better to have a few close confidantes like Viola and Marissa than a huge entourage that would scatter when the wind blew the wrong way. Coming to the reunion wasn't the painful experience I'd feared, and more than that, it taught me about the person I wanted to become. I gave Marissa a hug.

"What was that for?"

"Just because. We haven't known each other for long, but I'm so glad you're the one marrying my brother."

"Aww..." She blushed, then grinned. "Will you be a bridesmaid? We don't have a date yet, so if it clashes with filming and you can't, then I'll—"

"I'd love to, and I'll be there. I'll be by your side for the dress fitting, the cake tasting, the stripper show at the hen night, and the whole 'I do' part."

My brother choked on his beer. "Steady up there. Stripper show?"

Marissa went from rose-pink to scarlet as she gave him a

worried glance. "Maybe we could skip the strippers? How about a spa day instead?"

"You're no fun." But we all knew I was joking. "I'll start looking at spas."

"There's a nice one in—" Her phone rang, and she fumbled it out of her tiny purse. "Why is Janie calling so late?"

Janie was her sister. I'd met her a handful of times over the past year, but only briefly because she always seemed to be in a hurry. I was amazed that she was still awake at this time—if I had to look after two kids and a husband who never seemed to lift a finger to help, I'd have keeled over from exhaustion hours ago. Marissa wandered off to take the call, and I sagged against Owen.

"You okay?" he asked softly, pressing a kiss to my hair.

"I am. I really am. Until now, I didn't realise how much I needed closure. The prom seemed like such a big deal when I was eighteen, but it was just one day. The part I'd most been looking forward to was seeing you." I kissed him back, possibly a little too enthusiastically for public consumption, and Liam made a gagging noise behind me. I turned and stuck my tongue out. "Shut up, fartface."

"How do you feel about getting out of here?" Owen asked.

"Let's go."

Liam raised an eyebrow. "Is this where I do the 'you'd better take good care of my sister' talk?"

I elbowed my brother in the side. "That won't be necessary. Owen's taking *very* good care of me."

"Yeah, so I didn't actually need to know that."

But before we could find our coats and escape, Marissa came back, and she looked kind of shell-shocked.

"What's wrong?" Liam asked, quickly serious again.

"Janie just left Steven."

"Left him where?"

"No, *left him*, left him. Like, she's talking about hiring a lawyer and getting a divorce."

"What the hell? The guy's a prick, but I thought she was staying for the kids?"

"Well, she was crying a lot, so some of the details got lost, but I think she found a condom wrapper in his trouser pocket."

"And she's on birth control?" I guessed.

"She had her tubes tied after Alfie was born."

"Where is she?" Liam asked. "Where are the kids? Did she take them to your parents' place?"

"She didn't want to wake Mum and Dad, so the three of them are sitting on our doorstep. Harry's upset because his Nintendo battery's about to run out."

I patted my brother on the shoulder. "Best of luck."

Owen was slightly more sympathetic. "Anything we can do to help?"

"Unless you're offering to castrate Marissa's brother-in-law, I think we've got it covered for tonight." Liam sucked in a breath and let it out slowly. "Guess we should head home."

We said our goodbyes, collected our coats, and headed for the door.

"Don't forget your goody bags!" Lauranne Milner-was-Smith called, running after us. "Serena, it was so great to see you tonight, and Owen. I wasn't sure you'd come after...you know."

"It's all in the past."

"Hopefully, you'll both come again next time?"

"Next time?"

"We're already planning another get-together—we're hoping to hold them every five years from now on—and maybe we'll do something for the kids as well? So many people are getting married and starting families." She cut her gaze towards a lonely Libby, standing by the stage with a glass of wine in her hand. Was she meant to be drinking that? What about the baby? "Some of them are even staying married."

"We'll see what our schedules look like."

"Oh, yes, you'll be busy jet-setting, I suppose. They haven't really killed off Detective Cartwright, have they? She's my favourite."

"I couldn't possibly say."

We finally made it into the car. A sleek black Mercedes, complete with chauffeur. Owen had known all along that I would go to the reunion, and it had been waiting in the driveway. Sometimes, I thought he knew me better than I knew myself. It was a long drive back to Broxbourne, but before I could roll up the privacy screen and raise the possibility of a little naughtiness in the back of the limo—something I'd been contemplating all evening—it was my turn to get a phone call.

And my guts seized when I saw the name on the screen.

Dylan Young, producer of *Whispers in Willowbrook*. Why was he still working at eleven p.m.? I was tempted to send him to voicemail, but just knowing there was a message would ruin the rest of the evening. He really did have a terrible sense of timing.

"Dylan, how are you?"

As usual, he didn't bother with preamble. "Serena, I just got off the phone with Marc di Gregorio's agent."

"Oh?"

"Marc has expressed an interest in guest-starring on the show next season. I assume you discussed it with him?"

No, not a word. But I didn't want to sound like an idiot.

"He's a huge fan of *Whispers*, and I told him I loved working on it."

"Good, good. It'll be quite a coup if we can get him, but

he's insisting the two of you share screen time, so I'm going to need you to sign a new contract by the end of the week. I trust that won't be a problem?"

"Uh... I'll need to discuss it with my boyfriend. It would mean us spending time apart, and—" Owen must have been able to hear the conversation because he mouthed, "Do it." "And it's a big commitment. But as long as we can make the logistics work, then I'd love to be involved for another season."

"Have your agent call my people in the morning."

"I will." Dylan hung up without saying goodbye—again, not unusual—and I was left staring at the phone. "Did Marc just get me my job back?"

Owen brought my hand to his lips and kissed my palm. "It does seem that way. I wanted to hate the man, I really did, but I can't."

"You have nothing to worry about. I like Marc, but I love you." I closed my eyes and breathed out the last of my worries. The future stretched in front of me like a dream. "And now it's time to celebrate. Is there any more champagne?"

The car had a mini fridge hidden in the armrest, and Owen fished out two small bottles. I rummaged through the goody bag in case there was any chocolate and came out with a single heart-shaped truffle, a Fairoaks Grammar Valentunion keyring, and a packet of imitation Haribo.

"Gummy bears?" Owen asked hopefully. While it was always me who'd had the sweet tooth, he'd never been averse to stealing my candy.

"Gummies, Valentine edition." I tipped a selection into my hand. The best part? They were all red. "We have bears, hearts, rings, lips, and...I'm not sure what this is. A wine glass?"

"I think it's meant to be a rose."

I preferred the real roses he'd brought me this morning, along with a card and breakfast in bed. Not that I'd eaten the croissant. No, it had been crushed under Owen's arse when I got distracted by something even more delicious. Did I mention that he'd served breakfast naked? This was the best day ever.

Owen picked out a ring, and then he got the funniest look in his eye.

"What?" I asked. "Are you sad it doesn't fit?"

"I don't know. Why don't you try it on?"

Giggling, I tried to wedge it onto my finger, but it got stuck halfway. "It's a bit tight. Here, take a nibble and maybe it'll stretch."

But Owen didn't bite. No, he just fidgeted, and why did he look so nervous?

"Marry me, Serena."

Oh, that was why.

Wait...*what*?

"Wait a second... Did you just...?"

"Yes."

Boom. That was the sound of my ovaries exploding. We'd been dating for less than a month, and my whole life had been flipped on its head, but who cared? This was Owen, and he was asking me to stay by his side forever. To be his wife. To have him and hold him, till death do us part. There was only one answer I could give.

"I'm going to need a ring that isn't biodegradable."

"Is that a yes?"

"Of course it's a yes, you idiot. And in line with our policy of honesty and openness, I should tell you that I took my knickers off in the bathroom before we left. How do you feel about limo sex?"

Wordlessly, he unclipped my seat belt and pulled me onto his lap.

"Is that a yes?" I asked.

His grin was positively filthy. "What do you think?"

"I think this is the most fantastic Valentine's Day I've ever had."

Owen nuzzled my ear. "Happy Valentine's Day, not-quite-Mrs. Cadwallader."

"Happy *first* Valentine's Day, Mr. Almost-Carlisle. We're going to have plenty more."

Bonus Chapter

AXES AND APPLEJACK: A FEW THOUGHTS FROM EMMY

Curious how Emmy's fight with Ros unfolded? So was I, so I wrote a bonus scene for the folks in my reader group.

Download your free copy here:
www.elise-noble.com/axes

What's Next?

The next book in the Happy Ever After series is Janie's story, A Very Happy Halloween...

Always trust your heart? Codswallop.

In her teens, Janie Osman learned that bad boys are bad news. Fun was overrated, and mundanity became her new goal—two kids, a part-time job, an unremarkable husband, and a deep and meaningful relationship with her battery-operated boyfriend. Only for it all to get torn away in an instant.

A move to the cosy village of Engleby seems like the best option, but rebuilding her life isn't easy, especially with two young boys in tow. When a random act of vandalism brings trouble into her life in the form of Eisen Renner, the ultimate bad boy, will she follow her head or her heart? Should she choose security? Or risk everything for love?

For more details:
www.elise-noble.com/hh

My next book will be the seventeenth Blackwood Security novel, *The Devil and the Deep Blue Sea*...

It all started with a turtle and a pair of designer sunglasses...

A bodyguarding gig in the Caribbean? Living the dream, right? Former Navy SEAL Knox Livingston soon finds out the trip is no vacation. Pop princess Luna Maara is a pain in everyone's ass, including the local judge's. When Luna finds herself sentenced to a month of community service at a turtle sanctuary, Knox hopes she might finally rethink her behaviour, but little does he know, the nightmare is only just beginning.

Caro Menefee moved to Valentine Cay to escape her past, and the last thing she needs is a rich brat and her entourage invading the peaceful paradise. Although Knox and his equally cocky buddy sure are pretty to look at. And that's all she's going to do: look. She swore off men before she left California, and she has quite enough to worry about without adding two toned six-packs into the mix. The turtle population is declining at an alarming rate, and she's not convinced it's all down to natural causes. Will Knox help or hinder her quest to save a species? And will Caro join the turtles on the endangered list?

For more details:
www.elise-noble.com/deep-blue

133

If you enjoyed *A Very Happy Valentine*, please consider leaving a review.

For an author, every review is incredibly important. Not only do they make us feel warm and fuzzy inside, readers consider them when making their decision whether or not to buy a book. Even a line saying you enjoyed the book or what your favourite part was helps a lot.

Want to Stalk Me?

For updates on my new releases, giveaways, and other random stuff, you can sign up for my newsletter on my website:
www.elise-noble.com

If you're on Facebook, you might also like to join Team Blackwood for exclusive giveaways, sneak previews, and book-related chat. Be the first to find out about new stories, and you might even see your name or one of your suggestions make it into print!

And if you'd like to read my books for FREE, you can also find details of how to join my advance review team.

Would you like to join Team Blackwood?

www.elise-noble.com/team-blackwood

facebook.com/EliseNobleAuthor
x.com/EliseANoble
instagram.com/elise_noble
goodreads.com/elisenoble
bookbub.com/authors/elise-noble
tiktok.com/@EliseNobleWrites

Also by Elise Noble

Blackwood Security

For the Love of Animals (Nate & Carmen - Prequel)

Black is My Heart (Diamond & Snow - Prequel)

Pitch Black

Into the Black

Forever Black

Gold Rush

Gray is My Heart

Neon (novella)

Out of the Blue

Ultraviolet

Glitter (novella)

Red Alert

White Hot

Sphere (novella)

The Scarlet Affair

Spirit (novella)

Quicksilver

The Girl with the Emerald Ring

Red After Dark

When the Shadows Fall

Phantom (novella)

Pretties in Pink

Chimera

The Devil and the Deep Blue Sea (2024)

Blue Moon (2024)

Blackwood Elements

Oxygen

Lithium

Carbon

Rhodium

Platinum

Lead

Copper

Bronze

Nickel

Hydrogen

Out of Their Elements (novella)

Blackwood UK

Joker in the Pack

Cherry on Top

Roses are Dead

Shallow Graves

Indigo Rain

Pass the Parcel (TBA)

Blackwood Casefiles

Stolen Hearts

Burning Love (TBA)

The Trouble Series

Trouble in Paradise

Nothing but Trouble

24 Hours of Trouble

The Happy Ever After Series

A Very Happy Christmas

A Very Happy Valentine

A Very Happy Halloween (2024)

Standalone

Life

Coco du Ciel

Twisted (short stories)

Books with clean versions available (no swearing and no on-the-page sex)

Pitch Black

Into the Black

Forever Black

Gold Rush

Gray is My Heart

Audiobooks

Black is My Heart (Diamond & Snow - Prequel)

Pitch Black

Into the Black

Forever Black

Gold Rush

Gray is My Heart

Neon (novella)

A Very Happy Christmas

A Very Happy Valentine (2024)

Dirty Little Secrets

Secrets, Lies, and Family Ties (2024)

Made in United States
Troutdale, OR
12/26/2024

27299609R00089